THE CASE OF THE RUSSIAN CHESSBOARD

A Sherlock Holmes mystery only now revealed

By Charlie Roxburgh

Paperback ISBN 9781780922164
ePub ISBN 9781780922171
PDF ISBN 9781780922188

Published in the UK by MX Publishing
335 Princess Park Manor, Royal Drive, London, N11 3GX
www.mxpublishing.com

Cover design by
Kristina and Cameron

Cover layout and construction by
www.staunch.com

Contents

Acknowledgements

Stating the obvious, this story is wholly overshadowed by debt to the genius of Sir Arthur Conan Doyle for creating the whole genre of the Sherlock Holmes story and its perennial key characters - without which this tale would never even have been conceived.

Nor could this story have been possible without much inspiration from historical accounts, for instance concerning the Russian Czar's security services or the anarchist communes of Victorian Essex. You could not make some of these strange things up – and this story hasn't.

Another source for background colour has been the 1903 novel, *A Girl Among the Anarchists*, by Isabel Meredith, who actually forayed into the Russian political exile scene in late Victorian London, where *The Case of the Russian Chessboard* is set.

Amidst all this derivation and inspiration by others, at least the plot is wholly original fiction!

Special thanks to Kristina and Cameron for creating the cover design.

Chapter 1: An Ominous Message

There were many dark mysteries which I saw unravelled during my long partnership with Sherlock Holmes. But few imbued me with such a profound sense of dread as the case which began with an unexpected caller late one gloomy November afternoon. The doorbell had rung downstairs, followed by rapid footsteps on the stairs. "Hallo, what's this?" said Holmes, "We have no appointments."

He strode out to the landing and soon ushered in a young woman with dark hair, perhaps 25 years in age, soberly dressed in grey.

She struck me as studious-looking, perhaps a librarian, someone who knew well a sheltered, gentle world of books. But her face was silently screaming a mixture of fear and grief. She was clutching a newspaper tightly to her chest.

Holmes showed her to the vacant chair.

"Mr Holmes," she exclaimed quickly, "I am so sorry to call on you unexpectedly like this. But I am utterly desperate and no-one but you can help with a peculiar and terrible problem." She looked at Holmes very directly, as if summoning up all her determination that he help her.

"Madam, I can see that you are troubled," said Holmes gently, "as are so many people when they first call on my services. This is my colleague, Dr Watson, before whom you can speak as frankly as before myself."

"My name is Victoria Simmonds," said our visitor, recovering composure for a moment. Then she gasped and looked closer than ever to tears. "I need help to save my sister. From whatever is going on in the house from which she has just sent me the most shocking message. To save her from whatever nameless horror has just driven this friend of ours to her death."

She thrust forward her newspaper to us. It was the evening paper and just half an hour earlier I had read the very page she showed. A young woman had thrown herself under the wheels of a heavy locomotive, pulling in to Euston Station. She had died horribly in full view of people standing screaming on the platform from which she had just leaped. She had been identified by a Russian passport found on her mangled body. The police were asking for anyone who knew her.

"This is Sophia, who was a friend of both my sister, Angela, and myself. She was living at Liberty House, the very same hostel to which my sister, Angela, has just now moved."

Victoria Simmonds paused, swallowed and continued.

"Yesterday Sophia suddenly turned up at my apartment in Bloomsbury, weeping and weeping. I was most surprised to see her because I believed that she had just recently departed for Russia. She begged me to let her stay the night, just one night, because she was desperate to avoid Liberty House, which has been her dwelling place in London. I asked her what was wrong there but she begged me not to make her talk about it now. She would tell me in the morning, she said. And Liberty House is where my sister Angela has now gone to live". A wave of pain crossed her features and she seemed again close to tears.

She continued. She had seen no point in pressing Sophia, whose English was limited. So she waited till the morning. Throughout the night she had kept waking to the sound of Sophia weeping in the room next door – waves of convulsive weeping which increasingly alarmed our client. Around five in the morning, Victoria Simmonds had at last fallen deeply asleep. When she finally arose, she found that her guest had already left the apartment.

"So you got no explanation for her distress? Did she leave no note?" queried Holmes.

"Actually, she did leave a note. But it wasn't for me. It was addressed in Roman alphabet, for my benefit, to another Russian woman, whom we all know. But the message itself was in Russian alphabet, just one line long. Since I could not understand it, I did not know whether it would be useful to bring it."

Holmes seemed suddenly to look at her closely. "I see quite some possibility that it could be useful," he said. "I could arrange translation by a very discrete person."

7

Victoria Simmonds continued her account. "So I went off to do some teaching – I give tuition in biology at a women's college. And on my way home..." Her face seemed once more wracked with pain. "On my way home I saw this." She struck the newspaper like it was a hateful enemy. "And then when I got home I found a note from my sister Angela telling me she was now moving into Liberty House for good. She has been living on and off in my apartment but also staying for weeks at a time at Liberty House, the whole last fortnight in fact. And her message chills me to the bone. I cannot help but fear that it's linked to whatever caused Sophia to throw herself before that train." She looked at Holmes very directly, desperation in her eyes.

"Have you brought this other note?" Holmes asked.

"I have indeed," she said, passing him a folded note. "Please read it for yourself. For I have read it myself too many times already."

She sighed, tears in her eyes. Holmes read out the note slowly.

" 'Dearest Victoria, I must say farewell forever. Events have occurred which have called me on a path on which there is no going back. You would not know me now nor want to know me. For your own good, you must never, never come near Liberty House again nor seek to learn one shred of information further. Treat me as one

8

already dead and mourn, if needs be, for the sister you once had. For my part, I greet with steely resolve whatever must be my fate. The gates of hell are opening for me but I stride forward without flinching, like a fighter already condemned to death, for whom the worst has already happened.

I have taken with me now my passport and the few things of mine which I still need from the apartment. Do what you wish with the rest. My key you will find under the letterbox.

Whatever you do, you must stay away. Thank you for everything.

Farewell

Angela'"

We sat in utter silence for a moment. The coal fire sputtered in the grate. Through the window on to Baker Street the darkening foggy sky cast sepulchral gloom.

Holmes pursed his lips: "Most ominous, it seems. Does Angela's message make any sense to you?" Our client shook her head.

"Concerning Sophia's grim death, we should not make assumptions too readily," said Holmes. "We do not know from what she was fleeing when she leaped before that train. Whether it was from an unnoticed pursuer or from some dreadful situation, maybe at Liberty House, whose pain she could no longer bear. Translation of Sophia's note may shed some light."

He looked at Miss Simmonds: "Have you responded to the police call for people who knew Sophia?"

"Mr Holmes, I need to save my sister. I came to you as a private detective". She stressed the word 'private'. "If I talk to the police, they'll make a bee-line for Liberty House and goodness knows what Angela might then get caught up in." She looked imploringly at Holmes.

Holmes' eyes narrowed. "I think, Miss Simmonds, it would help me to hear how your sister got involved with this Liberty House."

It had begun, it transpired, with Victoria Simmonds attending a talk at Hampstead Public Library, organised by the Society of Friends of Russian Freedom. She had felt captivated by a dynamic young Russian woman who was describing oppression by the Czar's government in Russia. She brought her sister Angela to another talk. They had spoken afterwards to this woman, Anna Perovskaya, who then invited them first to one, then more meetings amongst London's community of

Russian exiles and their English supporters. It was in fact to this Anna Perovskaya that the note was addressed, which Sophia had left in Victoria Simmonds' apartment soon before she was crushed under the train.

"Can you help me understand what fired your interest in all these Russian meetings?" Holmes inquired.

She paused for a moment's thought. Holmes' question seemed to help her compose herself.

"For some years now," she replied, "both Angela and I have followed a strong desire to free ourselves from all the ideas, customs and prejudices which permeate the class of society in which we were raised. We have both, for instance, pursued education with a vigour which is commonly discouraged among women and likewise have made ourselves financially independent as teachers. We are keen to combat all ways of thinking, which subjugate people, whether in Britain or in other countries. The people's struggle in Russia is perhaps the sharpest instance in the world today of the fight against backward ideas."

Now I am an old military man and a doctor too and there was something about the social world, which Miss Simmonds then began to describe, which rather roused my hackles. It seemed a mixture of all sorts of people who wouldn't toe the line in whatever country they came from – or who liked to make out that they didn't toe the line.

11

At these meetings there were exiled Russian nihilists, rich English liberals who sympathised with the underdog anywhere but home, English Socialists, bluestocking feminists and would-be poets and bohemians of all nationalities - and various Italian and Spanish anarchists on the run from their own governments. From the Society of Friends of Russian Freedom there seemed to spread out all sorts of study groups, reading circles, tea-parties and soirées for intellectuals in Hampstead and Chiswick and goodness knows what else. To my grumpy mind they sounded like an audience excitedly following revolutionary dramas from their own perfectly safe seats in the theatre of life.

But Sherlock Holmes gently drew a tale out of Miss Simmonds. He seemed to lift her mood somewhat by asking questions about the people she mentioned. It took our minds away from harsh horrors here and now – a young woman's body hideously mangled under a locomotive's wheels and another young woman striding towards a yet nameless fate.

From Victoria Simmonds' account, Anna Perovskaya attracted admirers like a magnet. Anna and Angela had become close, which had thrilled Angela and made Victoria a little jealous. Anna had introduced Angela to a hostel and centre for Russian political exiles, which was called Liberty House. It comprised two brick terraced houses, next to each other, rented from a slum landlord in a mean side-street in Camden Town – less than an hour's walk across Regents Park from Baker Street.

Anna Perovskaya had started it and obtained the rent from a charitable fund created by Count Kropotsky, the well-known Russian exile.

Indeed, the white-bearded, avuncular Count cut quite a figure in London in those days and I kept reading about him in the newspapers. He rallied together wealthy British donors to support charities for Russian exiles and had made the anti-Czarist cause rather fashionable.

Our client had visited Liberty House only twice, long ago, and had felt uncomfortable at the roughness of the place. There were usually a dozen regulars living there. Three times a week they provided free lunches followed by political discussions for anyone who wanted to come. One of the large upstairs rooms held sewing machines for volunteers to make dresses to raise money. Miss Simmonds said something about these Russian radicals' communes always having such a dressmaking room. It was something to do with making men do the same work as women, but I could not quite make sense of it. Holmes however seemed to grasp all her talk with ease.

The residents, she said, were Russian exiles but visitors included Italian, Spanish and English anarchists and discussions were often conducted in broken English. An older, well-educated Russian, called Ivan Myshkin, ran the political discussions. Our client had found him as off-putting as she found Anna Perovskaya exciting and inspiring. He seemed stuffy and too full of his own knowledge.

Victoria Simmonds said that her sister now often lived at Liberty House for weeks at a time as a volunteer helper. Angela was working hard at learning Russian and seemed to have become deeply committed to the anti-Czarist movement.

"Were you aware of anything that troubled her there?" asked Holmes.

"Nothing whatsoever which could explain her note," replied Victoria Simmonds. "But some months ago she got upset about some terrible quarrelling at Liberty House and I remember feeling glad I'd stayed away.

"Anna had been away on her frequent travels and a wild-sounding young Russian nihilist had started coming to their lunchtime discussions. Everyone was in awe of him because of some daring escape from a Russian prison. Angela said he took over the meetings to mock Ivan Myshkin's political talks as feeble and boring. He told them that better revolutionary training would be to conduct street robberies on the wealthy people up the hill in Hampstead. That way they could learn to enjoy danger, cultivate hate for rich people, and raise funds."

Victoria Simmonds shuddered and continued: "He sounded like a nightmare anarchist thought up by a Tory newspaper. But Angela said he skilfully made Ivan Myshkin look weak and fussy, while playing the forceful man of action himself. He always carries this length of chain, she said, which he would brandish like a flail to show the violence which he says the true revolutionary must cultivate. And he was trying to take over as leader, Angela said."

But Anna Perovskaya had then returned. She had quickly organised a vote and the newcomer was banned from entering Liberty House again. But Angela hadn't been sure which way younger residents would have voted, if Anna not had been there to back Ivan.

"What was his name?" asked Holmes, poised with a pencil and notepad. "Why, it was Pyotr Bogdanovich, I recall," said Miss Simmonds. "Why do you ask?"

"We need all information possible if we are to fathom the meaning of your sister's note, which I would like to keep, if I may, for study," said Holmes in a sombre voice. "Tomorrow I will make enquiries about Liberty House from a discreet and well-informed acquaintance within the Russian exile community. A visit to him will take me a whole day. The day after tomorrow, please come here again at ten in the morning. And please bring Sophia's note."

"Mr Holmes, Mr Holmes, do you think you can save my sister from…whatever can be going on in that house?" asked Victoria Simmonds, her voice trembling. "Angela has told me that I must never find out. Sophia simply wept and wept and then killed herself. You are the only person whom I can turn to. Had Anna Perovskaya been here, I could have gone to her. But she is away on business at Tallinn on the Baltic Sea. I am utterly desperate."

"I am reasonably confident that we will find at least part of the explanation," replied Holmes. "But whether I can save Angela I cannot yet say. Nor whether you may not regret learning whatever explanation I eventually bring you. Remember, she has warned you not to find out."

"I cannot leave her. It was I, after all, who first drew her into this," said Victoria Simmonds. Her voice grew more agitated. "She is my little sister. Her note tells me that I will never see her alive again. I must do everything I can to save her." Suddenly she looked pained by her own display of emotion and halted, silent.

"You have my word of honour," said Holmes slowly, solemnly, "that I will do my utmost for your sister."

"Thank you, Mr Holmes," she said softly, her eyes lowered. Then swiftly she rose and left.

We sat momentarily in silence as the sound of the client's steps receded down the stairs.

The sky was dark now and rain pattered on the windows. Snug by the coal fire, I pondered what strange tragedy might be unfolding this very moment, just the other side of Regents Park. But Holmes was donning his overcoat, cape and hat.

"Going out in this weather, my dear chap?" I asked him.

"Just a quick look at a certain back street in Camden Town, where at least some answers must lie. Though we must approach very cautiously."

"But in this dark and rain?"

"Just the time for oil lamps and signs whether people are at home. And the worse the weather, the easier to spot the other thing I am looking for."

"What is that, Holmes?"

"Other people who are watching Liberty House."

Chapter 2: A Strange World Opens Up

When I rose the next morning, Holmes had already departed on his mission. Myself, I set off to visit a cousin in Hertfordshire and did not return till eight in the evening. Holmes was back already, sitting in his armchair, wreathed in pipe smoke, like an Orthodox priest with a censer, eyes closed and enrapt in thought. On the floor beside my chair lay a strange pair of canvas sandals. Holmes opened his eyes.

"A present for you Watson, the sandals."

"I thought you were dealing with the Russian Empire, not the Roman Empire," I replied. "Why on earth get me sandals?"

"Sandals are something they make and sell for a living at the New Eden Colony. It's a curious new community in rural Essex for high-minded critics of our society and it gives shelter to Russian political exiles. It's where Grigori, my Russian informant, lives. He's given me hours of his time but private gifts are against this community's principles. So I bought the sandals to say thank you. New Eden people are back-to-nature folk who preach sandal wearing as part of correct living. So you can feel all goody-goody, Watson."

"What is this place, this 'New Eden'? And is the investigation going well?"

"It goes well in terms of learning from Grigori some important secrets," Holmes replied. "For it turns out that he knows about all three Russians mentioned by Miss Simmonds. And one of them actually tried to live at New Eden but got driven out for conduct which, even for these freethinkers, is beyond the pale.

"However, for the Simmonds sisters, the investigation is going badly. For Grigori's information casts a most sinister light on the case." Holmes sat himself upright.

"Grigori is a Russian exile, now in his forties, who all his life has fought the Czar's government. As a youth, he was printing forbidden pamphlets in secret communal houses for revolutionaries, like those from which, he tells me, the Camden Town Liberty House is painstakingly copied. He was in and out of prison and was then put on some sort of life-long house arrest in a bleak, remote town. But he escaped to Britain three years ago.

"I have found him a valuable source of knowledge for some of my cases, though he has said goodbye to Russian politics, I think, thanks to the New Eden Colony.

"New Eden is deep in the Essex countryside, first a train journey, then a ride in a pony trap, and then a long walk along the banks of the River Ingrebourne - with a gunmetal grey sky threatening me with a downpour any minute. It's a ramshackle collection of log cabins, built by British admirers of the ideas of that Russian novelist, Count Tolstoy – you know, the 'War and Peace' chap. Count Tolstoy preaches back-to-nature farming communities where everyone is equal, all property shared and people try to treat each other in a totally Christian way.

"There's about 30 English people and 20 Russians at New Eden. Half of the Russians are former political prisoners, like Grigori, who are there temporarily to recover from their terrible experiences. This is something which New Eden offers Russian ex-prisoners for a while."

Holmes paused for a moment and puffed on his pipe.

"You might call it a community of cranks – vegetarians, pacifists, and Christian anarchists, like the Tolstoy people, and atheist anarchists like Grigori, all hand in hand and living very simply in rough wooden cabins. But there seems a kindly atmosphere and it has done Grigori a power of good. He was worn out and bitter when I first met him - bitter at his treatment by the Czar's police and bitter at the amount of feuds and betrayal that seem to go on among Russian revolutionaries. But today all that seems gone and I wouldn't be surprised if he stays at New Eden for good.

"Now these New Eden people loathe any violence or political plotting. They believe they must change society peacefully through more and more little communities like their own. So, once he heard the names of the Russians I wanted to know about, Grigori wanted us to talk out of earshot in one of their dank greenhouses, where they grow tomatoes, lest we upset people."

"So what does he say about the Simmonds sisters' Russian chums?" I asked.

"Bad news, I fear. Grigori thinks that both Ivan Myshkin and Anna Perovskaya are secretly officers in the Russian Socialist Revolutionary Fighting Force. That's much the biggest, most formidable terrorist group behind all the trouble we keep reading about in Russia. They are trying to wear down the Czar's government by decades, if need be, of assassinating anyone important to the government. So they blow up the royal train, throw bombs into the Grand Duke's box at the Opera, shoot the prison governor on his way to work and so on. And of course they've assassinated one Czar already. So assassinations, assassinations and more assassinations is their single-minded focus.

"And behind a bookish, schoolmasterly exterior, one experienced planner of the more daring sort of assassination is none other than Liberty House's Ivan Myshkin. Grigori suspects he might be plotting something in safety in England, which other people in Russia will actually carry out. Grigori thinks that other people at Liberty House may not know this side of him, since he is very, very secretive. They may see only the stuffy schoolmaster side for which, as Miss Simmonds told us, he can easily get mocked.

"He's an odd chap, says Grigori, all head and no heart. He does not warm to the wild and free ways of living which excite most Russian nihilists – and they do not warm to him either. But his mental powers are prodigious, it seems. Give him a train to blow up and he can plan out everything. Design of the bomb, where to tunnel under the rail track, how to hide all the earth dug out and so on. And he can work out a timetable for it all and a budget and how to assemble everything they need. And they say that he always checks up afterwards how accurate his plans proved - for next time."

"Good heavens, Holmes," I exclaimed, "so this is the man who is now some sort of mentor to the younger Miss Simmonds in her volunteer work at Liberty House."

"Now Anna Perovskaya is a different kettle of fish," continued Holmes. "According to Grigori, the nihilist women all want to copy her, while the nihilist men all dream of becoming her lover. I would opine that Grigori himself has been smitten with her, the way he talks about how her dazzling blue eyes, golden hair and winning smile have drawn so many to the revolutionary cause. She must be 15 years younger than Grigori but he still seems to look up to her. She is tough as well as beautiful. She can bicycle at breakneck speeds, Grigori says, and caused a rumpus in Russia by publicly training young women in jujitsu wrestling.

"He says her magic also works on wealthy Russian exiles, from whom she raises money and passes it to people like Ivan Myshkin. She's often travelling round Europe, giving talks in the various languages she speaks. She even travels backwards and forwards inside the Russian Empire, though Grigori can't understand how she still gets away with this."

"Didn't Victoria Simmonds say that Anna Perovskaya had gone abroad on business?" I asked. "Oh, Holmes, now we know what sort of business that might actually be."

"Yes, and also departed from Liberty House is the third Russian, whom Miss Simmonds mentioned, the young nihilist ruffian Pyotr Bogdanovich," Holmes rejoined. "A pity, because I should have liked a run-in with him because he sounded so intriguing."

Would Holmes ever rue his words so much as this wish that Bogdanovich cross his path! For a dark day would very soon come when we would curse this doom-dealing demon from the depths of our souls.

"Grigori told me how Bogdanovich, as an ex-prisoner, had actually stayed at New Eden for a short while, then tried to recruit some of the other former Russian prisoners for a revolutionary organisation," Holmes continued. "It seems he seeks out places where Russian exiles gather and tries to recruit followers, like he did at Liberty House. But he got driven out by the New Eden women once they discovered his game. These pacifists' rules don't allow them to use force to drive people out, nor may they turn to the police. So they followed him around in complete silence simply all the time, until he could stand it no more."

"So is this Pyotr Bogdanovich yet another Russian terrorist organiser?" I asked Holmes.

He grimaced. "He certainly makes out he is. But Grigori has his doubts. Grigori says that Russian exiles in London all know of Bogdanovich because of his outrageous behaviour and his famous escape from prison. For some he's a true nihilist hero of the most ferocious sort. For some he's an utterly evil, destructive devil. And for some he's a fraud or a clown.

"Grigori says that Pyotr Bogdanovich dresses like the first nihilists did, 30 years ago, before Bogdanovich was even born, so as to scorn all social conventions. He has filthy long black hair and beard and usually a great dirty grey blanket thrown over his shoulder, high boots, little blue spectacles and a heavy walking stick. Grigori says that nowadays you couldn't walk for ten minutes in St Petersburg, looking like he does, before you were arrested as an obvious revolutionary. So while some Russian exiles find these looks bold and romantic, others think it ridiculous. Though they don't tell him so because of the terrible rages which he can fly into – and he's a big young man, handy with the chain flail which we've already heard about, and he worships hate and rage as a sort of life-blood of the true revolutionary. That, I think, was Grigori's message." Holmes spoke slowly, thoughtfully, cradling his pipe in his hands.

He continued: "Grigori says that Bogdanovich gets intense reactions from Russian exiles because he so closely resembles a notorious young terrorist, called Serge Nechaev, who 25 years ago nearly destroyed the revolutionary movement through his horrendous new doctrine of all-out hate, murder and destructiveness. Many revolutionaries quit in disgust that so many of their number had heeded Nechaev. He wrote his ideas down in detail and, Watson, here it is for you. It's translated for English would-be revolutionaries and has been printed and distributed by Bogdanovich himself, who clearly likes to link himself to Nechaev.

"This was the only copy left at New Eden, because these pacifists dismembered any they found for a very practical use in their earth closet lavatory."

Holmes passed me over a slim booklet. It was titled *Catechism of a Revolutionary.*

"Have a read sometime," he said, "and you may find it hard to believe that anyone could frame sentiments so evil. But this Nechaev recruited many young followers with these ideas. Not just because he was forceful, but because he seemed to belong to a powerful secret society called The Organisation, which sounded large enough to defeat the Czar. After Nechaev was imprisoned, most people concluded that he had faked the Organisation's existence in order to recruit followers. But Grigori says there are other Russians who like to believe that The Organisation did actually exist and may now be rebuilding itself. If Nechaev faked The Organisation, they say, why did the government lock him in an empty prison with 70 soldiers to guard one man?"

Holmes paused, frowned briefly, then continued.

"And that, Watson, is why this peculiar chap, Pyotr Bogdanovich, gets strong reactions when he acts like a second Nechaev and claims to get contacted by The Organisation. He made this famous escape from a Russian prison, Grigori told me. Bogdanovich was awaiting trial and behaving as a furious, defiant political prisoner, the perfect nihilist. One day the governor was making all the prisoners stand in the yard while he shouted abuse at them. And Bogdanovich broke ranks and rushed up to him and spat in his face. So the angry governor ordered for him 40 lashes with the knout.

"Do you know about the knout? It's huge, heavy Russian prison whip of hard, dried leather entwined with barbed wire to tear off flesh. Only a big, strong man like Bogdanovich can survive 40 lashes.

"But, the story goes, Bogdanovich immediately broke free from the guards holding him and spat in the governor's face again. So the flogging was increased to 100 lashes, a definite and horrible death, and Bogdanovich was locked in solitary for a week before it would be carried out.

"And then two days before the date for his flogging, he somehow escaped. He says it was The Organisation who led him from his cell at night and took him for days in a rowing boat along a maze of waterways through reed beds and marshes till he could cross westwards to Europe.

"Many people can't see how The Organisation could have survived. But he escaped alright."

"What does Grigori think?" I asked.

"He's puzzled and frightened by Pyotr Bogdanovich's escape. I think for some Russian exiles, like Grigori, Bogdanovich sounds like the revival of a nightmare from the past. Whereas for others, the reappearance of The Organisation is like a dream coming true."

"Goodness, Holmes, what a strange world this case is opening up for us," I exclaimed. "And how much of the bad news will you break to Miss Simmonds when she comes here tomorrow?"

"Oh, that's another thing, Watson. She's not well enough to travel here. A cabbie delivered a note that she is indisposed and could we visit her at home, same time, instead. I would like you to accompany me...." Holmes paused.

"It's perfectly natural for private detectives to do home visits, just like you doctors. Nevertheless from now on it seems sober common sense that, anywhere we go during this case, you bring your revolver with you. And with all six chambers loaded."

Chapter 3: A Plan is Formed

The following morning we set off to Miss Simmonds' apartment in Bloomsbury.

"I was out late last night to observe Liberty House again," Holmes told me after we had climbed in the hansom cab. "Both nights there have been faint lights evident. This dwelling is our one strong link to the case and we may need to use it. I worry that that they might suddenly depart goodness knows where.

"There is a notice in English on one door saying 'Closed till further notice'. And another notice in Russian script, which might mean the same.

"Something new last night. There were three little pieces of red rag tied to the door knocker. It could be a signal. But to whom?"

"Did you see any of sign of the watchers, whom you said you were looking for?" I asked.

"There was no-one in the street itself," Holmes replied, "though I cannot say whether another house in the street might not have been rented for observing Liberty House".

"Good heavens, Holmes. So this case is grave enough to occasion such trouble? Who do you think could be watching Liberty House?"

"We now know there are ample grounds for Scotland Yard to do so. Also there may be rival revolutionary groups. And then, with most motive of all, there is the Okhrana, the dreaded secret political police of Imperial Russia."

"But this is Britain, Holmes, not Russia."

Holmes slowly shook his head. "In every major city in Europe there are officers of the Okhrana, who spy on Russian exiles there. And where there are many Russians, like Zurich and Paris, the Okhrana have many officers and agents. Some say that the Okhrana have the French police completely at their beck and call, enmeshed in a vast spider's web of conspiracy which spreads out from the Russian Embassy in Paris."

"How strong are the Okhrana in London then?" I asked, "There seem many Russians here."

"I don't know," replied Holmes. "But we may be finding out."

The cab passed through Bedford Square, then pulled up. Holmes struck the knocker on the door of Miss Simmonds' ground floor apartment. After a moment she opened up and ushered us into her sitting room, the first door on the left of the corridor.

It was a room with a thoroughly studious air. High bookshelves lined the walls except for the broad window and a gap in the bookshelves on the wall facing it, where a large tapestry, showing an Indian royal scene, was clumsily hung. It was folded to fit the space, cutting short the right side of a palace scene. The foreground was likewise obscured by a dressing table in the gap between the bookshelves so that the head of some Mughal emperor peered comically over the top of the mirror. So much for women science teachers, I could not help thinking, many a learned book but not the most basic womanly sense of artistic arrangement.

Holmes looked at the tapestry. "You have a liking for Indian style, Miss Simmonds?"

"Our parents are tea planters in India, Mr Holmes, and Angela and I were born there. But since I was 13 years old, both of us were sent to boarding school in England and our holidays were spent with an aunt."

Victoria Simmonds seemed emotionally more controlled than at our first meeting but most certainly not at ease. She seemed strangely remote compared to our first meeting, I thought. Had she, I wondered, had second thoughts about her sister's warnings against prying into whatever dark world she had entered?

Holmes got down to business: "Miss Simmonds, my Russian colleague, whom I've visited, can translate that short note in Russian from Sophia to Anna Perovskaya. May I take it with me when I leave?"

31

Victoria Simmonds looked startled. "Oh, Mr Holmes, I do not have it at hand. Oh, I am so sorry. Are you not able to help me without it?"

For a strange moment Holmes seemed frozen as if in sudden suspended animation. Then he was back to himself again.

"Well, Miss Simmonds, I have been thinking carefully and conclude that very soon we should attempt the most direct, obvious step for discovering what has been happening at Liberty House. Which is for you to try to talk to your sister.

"I know her note told you not to. But we need to act as soon as possible. She has taken her passport, according to her note to you, so presumably she may travel abroad. And, if she leaves Liberty House, how easily could we find her again?

"We need a safe way for you to meet her. We must heed her warning to stay away from this Liberty House. We need some twist which will get her to meet you elsewhere, rather than continue to refuse contact."

Holmes looked to Victoria Simmonds for reply. She nodded slowly a few times and waited for Holmes to continue.

"What say you, Miss Simmonds, to a messenger delivering a note to Angela at Liberty House which persuades her to meet you through a subterfuge like a message that your parents in India are seriously ill?"

"I can see how that could easily fail, Mr Holmes," Victoria Simmonds replied. "Angela has told me of a rule at Liberty House that all letters are owned in common and that all are read out to everyone. This got started while Pyotr Bogdanovich was trying to rule the roost. He told them that true revolutionaries have no private business and this idea of his outlasted his expulsion. I can imagine Angela trying to prove herself by saying she must overcome bourgeois ties of affection to our parents."

Holmes leaned forward. He seemed suddenly alert and urgent, like a ferret straining on a leash. "Then could you perhaps, Miss Simmonds, fabricate a message from Anna Perovskaya which requires Angela to meet you? Surely instructions from Anna would carry force with everyone at Liberty House?"

Victoria Simmonds seemed startled and aghast: "Oh, I simply could not do that. It is not possible."

Holmes changed tack: "Then could you write to Angela that you must sort out her share of some money or inheritance, before she disappears? I would surmise that, if the note is read out at Liberty House, she might find herself pressed by her companions to meet you so her money can be donated to their cause."

"You know, Mr Holmes," Victoria Simmonds replied, "I think you may be on to something with that. There is actually a substantial bequest from a great-aunt's Will which is shortly due to us. And I do think that the prospect of money would be welcomed at Liberty House, judging from pointed remarks during both my visits there."

"So now we need a safe place for you to meet her, not Liberty House," mused Holmes. Suddenly he leaned forward again with that alert, intense air: "Could you ask her here and maybe I could hide here and listen to what she said? If you wished, right now I could investigate your apartment for places for hiding myself for such a purpose."

A startled, very frightened look crossed Victoria Simmonds' face. "Oh no, Mr Holmes. I could not possibly agree to such, such a deception."

"Then how about asking her in your note to meet you at the entrance to Regents Park? Outside the gate to the Zoological Gardens, say? You could walk and talk with her in the Park, perhaps with a large umbrella." Holmes sat back, swiftly relaxed again.

A course of action was agreed. Victoria Simmonds would send a note by messenger before noon, mentioning her sister's inheritance and saying that she would wait beside the Zoological Gardens gate at ten o'clock the next morning. Holmes told her that, for her protection, he would watch from a distance for anyone who might have followed her sister. Then we would call at her apartment at four o'clock to learn what she had gleaned - or to discuss next steps, if no meeting had transpired. Holmes said that he expected she might feel too exhausted by then to visit Baker Street.

*　　*　　*

"Did she really need your 'private detective's home visit'?" I asked Holmes as we walked past the vendors of roast chestnuts outside the British Museum, after we had left Miss Simmonds' apartment. "To my doctor's eye, she seemed well, though under strain."

Holmes replied quietly: "Listening to her, Watson, I conjectured a shocking possibility, which I should not share with you for now, lest it be merely a disturbing chimera from my mind. I now think that home visits may be the only way that we will make progress with her.

"I shall not go back with you to Baker Street right now. This case is urgent and I must utilise the time before tomorrow's appointment. I shall visit the Reading Room here at the Museum and consult some tomes which may improve my understanding of the forces with which we may soon be at grips."

*　　*　　*

I stopped at a little restaurant off Marylebone High Street for a lunch of oysters, then headed back to Baker Street and spent the afternoon ordering my papers. Finishing early, I scanned through the pamphlet by Nechaev which Grigori had said that the young nihilist, Pyotr Bogdanovich, had been distributing in London. As Holmes had predicted, I found the attitudes in *Catechism of a Revolutionary* profoundly disturbing.

> 'A revolutionary is a doomed man. He has no personal interests, no feelings, attachments or property, not even a name....His purpose is only one: the quickest and most sure destruction of this filthy system. Merciless with himself, he must also be merciless with others. A single, cold passion for the revolutionary cause must suppress within him all tender feelings. Day and night he should have but one thought, one purpose: merciless destruction....The Organisation does not intend to impose on the people any new system. This will be the task of future generations. Our task is simply passionate, complete, and merciless destruction.'

So these were the words. Somehow that sinister Pied Piper, Nechaev, had set them to a tune which had captivated an army of idealistic young Russians. He had cajoled them to mayhem and murder and towards mass hangings on the Czar's gallows or slow death by despair in the prison camps of the freezing Siberian wastelands. And now his imitator, Bogdanovich, was seeking to play this tune again.

I fell into an uncomfortable, fitful sleep in my chair. I awoke clammy with sweat and uneasy and the vestiges of a ridiculous bad dream were fading from my mind. It may have been the oysters. And surely I had been thinking too much about all things Russian.

In the dream I saw a storybook Russian Easter scene of a church's golden onion domes against an azure blue sky and bells pealing. I saw the backs of black robed men, like Orthodox priests, walking in procession and chanting 'He is risen, He is risen' as the bells rang. Then I heard their chant of joy more clearly, 'Satan is risen, Satan is risen', and woke up in a restless cold sweat.

*   *   *

When Holmes returned, he seemed taciturn. Soon after supper, he prepared to leave the house again. Was he watching Liberty House again, I asked.

"It has to be done Watson," Holmes replied. "And there's more than Liberty House which needs watching now. It is hard work but it is now or never. Tomorrow we need a breakthrough. If Miss Simmonds has not drawn anything from her sister, I may try for a breakthrough by another means."

Chapter 4: House of Horror

At four o'clock the next day, promptly, Holmes struck the knocker on Miss Simmonds' front door. We were hopeful of progress because that morning, from a distance, Holmes had observed the sisters meeting outside Regents Park. He had departed when all appeared well.

But, when the door opened, for a moment I did not actually recognise Victoria Simmonds, so dazed and haggard did she now look. Plainly something appalling had recently occurred. She showed us to the same room as before. She sat for a moment quietly and the tears welled into her dark eyes.

"Oh Mr Holmes," she sighed, "I did meet my sister and she changed her mind and told me everything. And she has fallen into a hell so deep that no-one, no-one can rescue her now."

She sobbed convulsively. "My little sister is headed straight for the hangman, the black hood, the noose, the gallows trapdoor. And in whatever life is left for her before she is hanged, she has handed her body and soul for direction by a monster who is enmeshing her in the foulest, most terrible further crimes."

Suddenly she screamed aloud: "What can I do? Only the police can stop it now but they would just get Angela hanged sooner." She broke down in tears.

Holmes spoke gently but firmly: "Please Miss Simmonds, let me be the judge of what can be done."

Haltingly at first, Victoria Simmonds told her dreadful story. She had found Angela already waiting for her at the Zoological Gardens gate. They strolled off deep into Regents Park. After a brief, frosty discussion of their inheritance, Angela suddenly begged to unburden herself and they had walked for hours in the park while she told her tale.

"Around a week ago," Victoria Simmonds related, "All the regular residents of Liberty House, plus Angela, were sitting down to supper together, apart from Ivan Myshkin who had not yet returned home. And apart from Sophia, too, who had departed for Russia some days earlier.

"Suddenly there was a knock on the front door. One of them went to open it and in rushed Pyotr Bogdanovich, whom I told you about, and three other Russians. Two of them wielded revolvers, one had an axe and one carried a poker.

"They said they had orders from something called The Organisation to search the house for evidence that some residents of Liberty House were actually working for the Okhrana, the Russian secret police.

"They said that The Organisation had managed to infiltrate the Okhrana and had learned that supplies from the Okhrana were hidden in the house for the Okhrana's secret collaborators there. All that The Organisation knew was that they were kept somewhere under the floorboards in the dressmaking room.

"After argument and threats, the Liberty House people agreed to help with a search for something they didn't believe could be there. Eventually one of them did find a loose floorboard. Underneath it was a leather briefcase. The briefcase was locked so they cut it open and everyone crowded to see what was inside.

"There were two revolvers. Ammunition. There were British, French, Swiss and German banknotes. But it was the letter which stunned everyone. It was read out. Then passed round.

"Angela checked that she had understood the Russian correctly. It was on the notepaper of the Russian Embassy in London and was signed by a Russian Major who evidently was an officer of the Okhrana, the Russian secret police. And it was addressed to Ivan Myshkin.

"Angela said that she was too shocked by the revelation to take in all the details of the message. But one item was about an increase in Ivan's monthly pay from the Okhrana up to 400 roubles. Another item was that the Okhrana would instruct Count Kropotsky to continue funding Liberty House for another year. This too stunned everyone, Angela said, because Count Kropotsky was believed to be a sincere liberal, trusted by wealthy donors to run funds for exiled revolutionaries. But this revealed him too to be taking orders from the Okhrana.

"A final item caused turmoil the moment it was read out, Angela told me. It was that the Okhrana was halving its monthly pay to Boris Burtliev, another Liberty House resident, because of inefficient work for them.

"Boris Burtliev was actually standing there. He is a rather hopeless, heavy-drinking middle-aged Russian, says Angela, whom she always saw as a mere hanger-on. As soon as heard his name mentioned in the letter, this Boris ran for the front door but was chased and dragged back.

"Angela said he immediately began admitting that he was an Okhrana spy and was blubbering and begging for mercy, because death is the usual revolutionary punishment for such betrayal. He said he would tell everything - how he met this Okhrana Major every Monday in a little upstairs office in Clerkenwell, which had a sign saying 'Translation Bureau' and another sign which always said 'Closed'."

Victoria Simmonds started to weep again: "This is what is so terrible. Angela is trapped whatever happens. She told me she felt horrified that Ivan Myshkin was really an Okhrana agent and actually grateful to Pyotr Bogdanovich, of all people, for saving her from him.

"She told me that, talking privately to Ivan over some months, she had come mistakenly to trust and believe in him completely and that, secret from everyone else at Liberty House, she'd agreed to take part in a plot inside Russia. That's why she was learning Russian so hard.

"Ivan Myshkin wanted her to try for a post as a children's English private tutor living with one of the noble families in St Petersburg, who are close to the heart of the Czar's government. The idea was that she would pretend that she understood much less Russian than she has already actually learned. That way she could become a revolutionary spy and hear dinner table talk which revealed the plans and whereabouts of the people whom the revolutionaries seek to destroy. She has done some work as a private tutor and a governess in London, you see, so she has employers' character references for this sort of post.

"And now Angela had found that, according to Ivan's real plans, this private tutor plot would presumably mean her being fed false information by the Okhrana, so that revolutionaries were led into deadly traps."

Victoria Simmonds gazed ahead in silence for a moment. She continued:

"My sister actually appeared bright in a strange, terrible way as she talked about how Pyotr had saved her from a terrible mistake and had shown that it was he, not Ivan Myshkin, who could lead her on the true revolutionary path. She said that now she had seen the truth that, after all, Nechaev's Organisation had survived, just as Pyotr had said, and had actually managed to infiltrate the mighty Okhrana. The briefcase under the floorboards and Boris Burtliev's confession showed that Pyotr Bogdanovich was in touch with a powerful secret revolutionary organisation. Which meant that she could be in touch with it too, if she followed Pyotr.

"Then, Angela said, Pyotr had the traitor Boris Burtliev gagged and tied tightly to a chair away in a back room. He posted two men with revolvers to guard the house's front door, waiting for Ivan Myshkin's return. When Ivan arrived home, they grabbed him. He was pushed at pistol-point into the big room where Pyotr had everyone assembled and Pyotr clubbed him to the ground with a poker. Then Ivan too was tied tightly to a chair. And Pyotr held Ivan's letter in front of him but Ivan started arguing and saying it was a fraud. Pyotr Bogdanovich then struck Ivan in the mouth with the poker, smashing his teeth. Then he gagged him...."

Victoria Simmonds was weeping again, her head sunk in her hands. Every detail of what her sister had told her seemed most painfully etched on her mind.

"Pyotr told them each person must now tell Ivan what they thought of him. And some really shouted and cursed at him. One nihilist woman, Katya, actually spat again and again on the bound man, who up to then had been their colleague and leader.

"Pyotr then told them that they were now a revolutionary tribunal who must pass judgement on their former leader. He thought that Ivan should die and would go round each person in turn, to hear their view. And one by one, 'Death' was each person's response.

"Angela told me that she really meant it, it wasn't just because she was frightened of Pyotr. She's really aghast that Ivan Myshkin could be such a traitor, especially since she had been about to give her life to follow his plans.

"And then Pyotr said that, since everyone had passed the death sentence, everyone should take part in the execution. He said that one single pistol shot would not attract too much attention in the street. He opened one of the big revolvers from the Okhrana briefcase, put in a single bullet, then spun round the six revolving chambers. He said that each person in turn should press the pistol against Ivan's head, shout something which showed true revolutionary hate, and then pull the trigger. And he would cock the pistol and spin it's revolving chambers. And they would carry on till the revolver went off."

Victoria Simmonds was now sobbing profusely. "He told them to volunteer for the order in which they would pull the trigger. And that they should notice anyone who lacked commitment and hung back. What a torment of a choice! Katya went first and the pistol just clicked. Then someone else. Then Angela - and Pyotr told her to hold it firmly in both hands and aim just like she really meant it. And the revolver fired and there was Ivan Myshkin's blood and brains everywhere and my little sister is now a murderess. She has killed a man, old enough to be her father, whom she had come to trust with her entire future. And she's now going to hang and it gets worse and worse and worse."

She was racked with weeping. "Pyotr had some brandy brought in for them to toast the revolution and toast my sister for firing the shot. All this with Ivan's body still tied in the chair in front of them. Then Pyotr had them take a bloodcurdling group oath of loyalty to The Organisation. And they were all drinking brandy, Angela says, and chanting 'The Organisation lives!'

"And then he led them to Boris Burtliev, tied up in his room. Pyotr told him he could choose between death and joining The Organisation. When, surprise, surprise, he picked the latter, he was told to prove his newfound loyalty by cutting up Ivan's body for disposal. But he couldn't get far with it, even with brandy. And Angela thinks they may now have killed him in his room. It is one horror after another.

"No-one is yet allowed to go out without permission from the group. Angela had to get permission to see me and your idea about money worked at once.

45

"But some people have sneaked away. Angela's friend, Katya, volunteered to take Ivan's sawn-off legs in bags to the undergrowth on Hampstead Heath but then she never returned.

"While Pyotr was out, Sophia turned up unexpectedly, having apparently cut short her journey to Russia. She was told what had happened and left almost immediately, before anyone had thought what to do with her. And of course she then came to me in that terrible state but could not talk about it."

Victoria Simmonds paused and sighed deeply. One felt an urgency about her to share this dark world into which she was now plunged. I glanced at Holmes. He was gazing at her enrapt. On his face was an expression I rarely saw on him. It was a sad and tender expression, close to compassion.

Our client continued: "Angela sounded to me like she was just waiting for her fate, waiting to get it all over. Sometimes she was talking in this eerie bright tone about these terrible things which Pyotr's now preparing them to do. But then sometimes the horror of it seems to overwhelm her. She's getting hardly any sleep what with fear of what will happen next and Pyotr Bogdanovich making everyone have long late night group discussions.

"He is drinking a lot and his plans seem constantly changing. Some of the time he tells them he is waiting for orders from The Organisation about what to do next. He says The Organisation have told him to approach the Russian

Embassy and pretend to offer his services as a collaborator, as soon as they give him the signal.

"But then he tells them that he'll be returning to Russia and that before this they must make some attacks in London which will terrify the ruling classes world wide, like the way that anarchists in Spain throw bombs into rich people's boxes at opera houses. It is something which they call 'Propaganda by Deed'.

"Each person has got to present an idea for the most shocking attack they can think of. Pyotr says that the group will then choose which ideas it will carry out. He has been telling them that, by launching one attack after another, they can drown their fear through excitement. He says they must find terrorist ideas which really fire their imagination.

"It is things like rushing into the society jewellers, Aspreys, and killing as many as possible of the wealthy customers with their revolvers, axes and knives. That was one which Angela mentioned. Another idea was to start fires in Harrods at several places at once. And, can you believe it, Pyotr has been urging some attack on the Hampstead Marxist Study Circle because, by using too long words, it disdains the masses."

She gave a brief, bitter laugh. "And Angela and I used to go to their meetings."

"Other ideas were to throw bombs through the windows of wealthy homes in Belgravia," she continued, "or into the House of Commons from the public gallery to show Bogdanovich's rejection of bourgeois democracy. But they don't have any proper explosives. And, and..." She was finding it hard to get the words out. She began weeping again.

"And my little sister has gone and used her science education to help them make some. It's a nightmarish schoolboy concoction from medicine cabinet iodine and a household cleaning chemical, the only thing which can be made so simply. She first made it because Pyotr wanted something to blow up Liberty House if the police raided. That's something which revolutionary dens in Russia always have, a bottle of explosive on the mantelpiece to knock off and blow up the house if the police raid. But now Pyotr is pressing her to make more bottles for attacks in London. But she is terrified to make more because, once dried, it can explode with the slightest touch, she says."

Holmes nodded in recognition: "I know this fiendish substance. Indeed it would most likely explode if made in any quantity or moved around."

Her weeping became more powerful. "Maybe that's the best thing that could happen to Angela," she cried. "That the whole house blows up right now, before any more crimes, without any trace left behind, without our parents ever having to learn what she's become.

"Pyotr has been telling her that the biggest shock they could inflict on British society is if she committed an outrage herself, an educated bourgeois Englishwoman, not someone like him. But that she must make her own decision, because, unless she is truly firm in her heart, she will not be able to make a sufficiently menacing speech at her trial.

"He keeps telling her that she has a wonderful freedom because she's already due to hang for shooting Ivan and they can only hang her once. That she should get it into her head that she's going to die very soon, either on the gallows or from a policeman's bullet, and so she should use her remaining time in the most terrifying way that she can.

"But he has so many other jobs for which he needs her, because she's English, respectable-looking and she knows London. He's wanting her help for some dreadful thing which they are plotting against old Count Kropotsky, now they know he's in league with the Okhrana. He wants to force him to hand over the fund from which he finances exile groups. One idea is to force their way into Kropotsky's house in Hampstead, then torture him till he gives them the money." Victoria Simmonds buried her face in her hands.

"It is just one horrible plan after another, all garbled up and mixed with endless discussions and brandy drinking and

49

chopping up the last remains of the two Okhrana spies they've murdered. And Angela just seems blank and resigned, as if she is keen to get her life over and die for their appalling ideas. And I cannot see any vestige of any way out. Any action can only bring my sister to the hangman sooner rather than later or make her blow herself up with the rest of them. But maybe that's actually better than letting her soil herself with ever fouler crimes." She became overwhelmed by weeping.

"Miss Simmonds," Holmes said gravely, "at this very moment I cannot see a way out either. But, give me time to think through what we have now learned, and it is still possible that we may find some solution. I give you my word of honour to stand by you and to guard these ghastly secrets. I will do my utmost to achieve the best solution."

*   *   *

After we had left Miss Simmonds' apartment, Holmes and I walked silently at first along the dark Bloomsbury streets. A shocked, profoundly sombre mood had overcome us after what we had heard.

"Holmes, this is an utterly nightmarish situation in which both the Simmonds sisters find themselves," I exclaimed at last. "Now we understand what led that poor Sophia to throw herself under that train."

Holmes looked at me suddenly. "No, Watson, I do not think that we yet understand that at all. We have not learned why Sophia, who was not even present, should actually kill herself after hearing what we have heard today. No, Watson, there is some further hideous secret among the Liberty House people, which we have yet to unravel if we are to resolve this case. "

We walked a few steps in silence into a pool of soft yellow light from the next gas lamp. Holmes spoke again: "It seems to me that indeed we have mapped a dark cavern of hell in today's tale of murder, mad terror and young lives doomed to the gallows. But beyond it I sense a darker labyrinth still, which we have yet to explore. And in that inner labyrinth of hell lies the secret behind Sophia's mysterious death. Watson, I sense something stranger and more sinister yet to come."

Chapter 5: A Most Disturbing Proposal

Neither of us felt inclined to further conversation on the way back to Baker Street. My mood fluctuated. I felt appalled by the sheer ghastliness and hopelessness of the situation in which the Simmonds sisters had become entrapped, albeit through their own folly. I could not bear to contemplate what further, darker horror Holmes was now foreseeing.

Then I felt a mounting sense of panic at what fresh murderous crimes might very soon be launched from this house of the damned. Had Holmes been right to pledge secrecy to Victoria Simmonds? Should we not instead be heading straight to Scotland Yard so Liberty House could be stormed? I even wondered momentarily if I should not approach the police myself, if Holmes could not do something fast. Liberty House sounded like a barrel of gunpowder with a fuse burning beside it.

As we got home and were ascending the stairs, Holmes suddenly broke the silence.

"Watson, I forgot to tell you but I have a mysterious, short-notice appointment with a government bigwig in two hours' time and I would value your presence.

"Just before noon I received a note from brother Mycroft who, as you know, is chummy with the upper echelons of the Civil Service. He asked me to drop everything to give some urgent advice on some hush-hush matter to a civil servant called Malcolm Pryde-Anderson, who's some sort of rising star at the Home Office. I don't know any more but I always heed Mycroft. So I returned the note, agreeing to this Pryde-Anderson's invitation to his Club in St James this evening. Would it be a burden to accompany me?"

I did not perhaps reveal quite how relieved I felt for any distraction from the doomed world of the Simmonds sisters and the smouldering nightmare of Liberty House. When the time for our cab journey arrived, I was more than ready to escape.

Arriving in St James Square, we passed through the handsome white Palladian portico of Pryde-Anderson's Club. Holmes stated our business to the porter and we were shown to a spacious, elegant lounge with a grand red carpet. Sitting in a luxurious leather armchair under a sparkling chandelier, I contemplated the sheer grace and dignity of our surroundings. On the walls hung huge portraits of our most illustrious military leaders. Nearby us sat grave, distinguished-looking men with an air of seniority in government, military or colonial service. A few wore naval or army uniforms. More still had the bearing of senior officers.

Here was the cream of our Empire. Rightly, it was among such circles that Holmes' remarkable talents should be deployed, I reflected, rather than saving the Angela Simmonds woman from her deranged anarchist gang.

Malcolm Pryde-Anderson strode over to meet us. He was a short, florid-faced man with gold-rimmed spectacles and a dark waxed moustache and an air of busy activity and accomplishment. On a second glance, I realised he was surprisingly young – perhaps no more than 30 years old.

"Thank you indeed, Mr Holmes and Dr Watson, for coming at such short notice. Two colleagues have asked to meet you urgently and I shall shortly show you through to a private room where I will leave you with them. These colleagues are advising me for a highly confidential joint Working Party between the Home Office and War Office regarding national security."

Pryde-Anderson paused and pursed his lips as if thinking what to say next.

"Your assistance enables the Home Office to exchange favours with these two colleagues who are giving me valuable advice. So you should regard your kind assistance as an indirect service to the British government, a sort of *quid pro quo*, because they are actually diplomats from a friendly foreign Power. They are most helpfully advising us about advanced systems which they are developing in their own country. And in return they have asked for your urgent assistance."

Holmes stood up: "Would these diplomats by any chance hail from the Russian Embassy?"

"Good heavens, Mr Holmes, how did you deduce that?" replied Pryde-Anderson.

"Never mind that," said Holmes in a distant tone. "Let us hear what they ask. But I am not promising to do whatever they want."

Pryde-Anderson looked flustered, then annoyed. "But this is an inter-government *quid pro quo*, Mr Holmes. Most certainly, you had better think of Britain."

Quite curtly, he led us upstairs and ushered us into a sumptuously furnished, dimly lit, small sitting room. Heavy velvet curtains in midnight blue were drawn across the windows. An exquisite grandfather clock of finely polished walnut stood against the wall. Its lustrous mother-of-pearl clock face glowed softly like the moon.

With the words "Gentlemen, here is Mr Holmes and his assistant," Pryde-Anderson left us.

Eyeing us with interest from their armchairs were the two Russian diplomats.

One was an older man with a sallow complexion, long sideburns and straggly, greasy dark hair. He wore a purple velvet smoking jacket and a gaudy, richly embroidered, yellow silk waistcoat. Like some decadent aesthete, he was smoking a strong-smelling Turkish cigarette in a long tortoiseshell cigarette holder.

He was not my idea of a diplomat or even a proper Russian. He better resembled an ageing version of the more rakish sort of Eton prefect in a comic paper public school yarn. And, when we came to hear his faultless command of English turn-of-phrase, the impression was strengthened of a type of languid, arty Old Etonian whom I have never liked.

The other diplomat was younger and soberly dressed in a black suit. His blond hair was neatly combed-back and brilliantined and he sported a trim military-style moustache. He had cold little blue eyes. He too transpired to speak the sort of English which an expensive English boarding school education nowadays buys for the sons of wealthy foreigners.

Holmes sat down and opened conversation: "So you are officers of the Okhrana, our very own local Russian secret police."

"How nice to meet you, Mr Holmes, and how welcome that you recognise who we are," said the older man coolly, after a moment's pause. "So pleasant not to have to beat around the bush. I am Colonel Volkhovsky and this is Major Alexandrov." He turned flippantly to his colleague: "I say, Major, we've never had our diplomatic cover challenged so unceremoniously, have we?"

Colonel Volkhovsky turned back to Holmes. Suddenly his languid demeanour seemed gone: "Like you, I will get straight to the point. The Okhrana is in crisis. Somehow a hidden terrorist circle has infiltrated our force at a high level and is unmasking our agents within terrorist organisations, who are then being murdered. We hear you are investigating the red gang at Liberty House in Camden Town. Is that accurate?"

Both he and Major Alexandrov leaned forward and studied Holmes' face closely.

For a long moment there was silence save the ticking of the grandfather clock. Then Holmes nodded slowly in assent.

Colonel Volkhovsky continued: "We suspect that a key agent of ours, who has been leading and controlling that gang for us, has been unmasked and murdered. We have now lost all our secret collaborators in the gang and no longer know where it is heading. We fear it may be taken over by a mad nihilist terrorist of the most dangerous sort. There is now a chance of the most terrible type of bomb outrage – in London or wherever they may be going.

"You, Mr Holmes, are the only person who still has surveillance of this gang. For the sake of both Britain and Russia, we need you to work wholeheartedly with us to head off this deadly menace."

"Indeed, you make a compelling case for my assistance," replied Holmes calmly, "but I'd like to ask a couple of questions. How do you know about my investigation?"

I had been wondering this myself. It seemed startlingly inexplicable.

"We'll gladly tell you that, once you tell us who hired you," cut in Major Alexandrov.

"And the other question," countered Holmes, "is what you want me to actually do, if I agree to work for you?"

"First, that you tell us who hired you, everything you have found out, and exactly what you have reported to your client," said Colonel Volkhovsky. "Second, that on this case you henceforth work for us alone, though you pretend to continue working for your original client if we so decide.

"Third, that you and your assistant immediately accompany Major Alexandrov to St Petersburg for a secret briefing on the infiltration problem in the Okhrana.

"After that, we will plan the next steps together with you. And for this, we will pay you the very highest fees for your time."

Holmes stared impassively ahead for a moment, sphinx-like. Major Alexandrov scrutinised Holmes' face with his cold little blue eyes.

"If I do decide to help, I pledge to tell you within three days," replied Holmes.

"Three days, Mr Holmes!" Major Alexandrov exclaimed. "We need your information immediately to halt these mad anarchists from slaughtering innocents. Who hired you and for what purpose? Have you considered that you may be working for a terrorist agent without realising it? We know these Russians in London much better than you. Surely you must straightaway tell us who?"

"Mr Holmes, Mr Pryde-Anderson led us to expect a rather more helpful response," said Colonel Volkhovsky more calmly, "not least considering the help we are giving him."

"To be absolutely frank," replied Holmes, "I deserve time to think, because of the unfortunate reputation of the Okhrana here. We hear rumours how senior people in the Czar's own government fear that you actually run the terrorist groups which you proudly announce you discover. That it is those government officials who get in your way who are particularly likely to get assassinated by these revolutionaries. That, when the Okhrana chief goes on holiday, all the St Petersburg nobles seek seats on his train because this is the one train southwards which they know definitely won't get blown up. You've just told us that you were actually running a conspiracy at Liberty House. And you expect me to follow you without a second thought?"

I could not believe my eyes. At Holmes' mention of the train, both Russians seemed to be hiding grins behind their hands.

Colonel Volkhovsky sighed and rolled his eyes theatrically. "Mr Holmes, our methods may sound rather racy to, well, the boys in the fourth form. But I had expected a more adult sentiment from a man with your reputation. The viewpoint, which you've just presented, is really so last year, old chap.

"So let me explain our approach. I shall be extraordinarily frank with you because I sense that, deep down, you have the intellect to appreciate policies which step outside common men's ideas of good and evil. And we need to gain your wholehearted allegiance.

"Hunting terrorists is like finding needles in a haystack. Completely impossible. Unless you have a powerful magnet which draws those needles out of the haystack for you. And what is a magnet which will draw would-be revolutionaries out of the shadows? Why, it is anything which they might like to join - a thriving red bookshop, a club for radicals, somewhere like Liberty House, or an apparently successful terrorist gang.

"Sometimes we start these things ourselves. Or if we find them, we infiltrate them with revolutionaries who are really our secret collaborators.

"We move our secret collaborators into positions of power in these red organisations by arresting the people above them, clearing the way until our secret collaborators can step into leadership roles.

"Once we control one of these red circles, we nurture it like a poison tree. We help it grow in reputation to attract ever more enemies of the state, who thus unwittingly place themselves under our surveillance and command. Our secret collaborators propose terrorist acts so that we learn who has talent for terrorism.

"Then only very gradually do we harvest the fruit of our poison tree through arresting selected people. To arrest too many would destroy our magnet. Terrorists leave a group which looks doomed and then start one which we don't know about. To be effective, our magnets have to look successful.

"If we're being adult about it, Mr Holmes, we must allow most of our gangs' crimes to succeed or this system won't work. So we stop their most dangerous plots – and above all, we halt assassination plots against the Czar. As for the quota which we must permit - to be socially responsible, shouldn't we steer such assassinations towards those government figures who, frankly, prove poor team players in our modern approach to national security?"

"Yes, the socially responsible way to choose them," chimed in Major Alexandrov, nodding sagely.

"For instance," Volkhovsky continued, "say some political prisoners have died from floggings and the red rank and file are clamouring to assassinate a prison governor. Whom should we get our collaborators to suggest? Should it be a prison governor who always discreetly assists our requests to let our secret collaborators escape? Or one of those stuffy, self-centred governors who won't play ball with us just because escapes make him look inefficient?"

"If one of them has to, well, depart, the socially responsible choice is plain to see," murmured Major Alexandrov.

"And likewise among government Ministers," said Colonel Volkhovsky, "let's face it, there are patriots who support the Okhrana getting the extra funding it needs but also other Ministers who behind the scenes intrigue against us to the Czar."

"We know who they are," said Major Alexandrov, "we read all their private letters."

"So if we ever need to select an actual Minister, if say our revolutionaries are feeling aspirational, we do that likewise in a logical, socially responsible way. How else should we make our choice? Would you like us to draw names from a hat instead?" smiled Colonel Volkhovsky.

It was Major Alexandrov's turn to roll his eyes. "That would so lower the tone of the Okhrana's stage management of terrorism, Mr Holmes," he declaimed with poorly pretended indignation. "We take our responsibilities seriously. We sometimes have to choose between absolutely top drawer people, you know."

"So it's really rather cheap to make those boring old criticisms of the Okhrana, Mr Holmes," said Colonel Volkhovsky, "since, when one comprehends the full picture, our methods are as healthy and wholesome as a British butcher's dog."

I was feeling mocked. There was something much too clever-clever about them. But there was also a shocking logic to what they said, which one had not considered before. The image of Victoria Simmonds' distraught, tear-stained face flashed briefly into my mind. Were we going to place her fate in the hands of these aloof, supercilious men by following their instructions, as our Government seemed to expect?

The Okhrana officers were both sitting back now, eyeing Holmes smugly, as though they had forced the ball into his court.

"My apologies, gentlemen," said Holmes pleasantly, rather to my surprise. "You are indeed broadening my outlook. Pray tell me more. How do you get revolutionaries to work as your collaborators? What motivates them?"

Volkhovsky gazed thoughtfully at the ceiling: "We have actually tens of thousands of would-be revolutionaries on our payroll. Often it starts with us offering a deal whereby they work for us just a little to avoid jail in Siberia for themselves or for a close friend or a dear relative, whom we have caught red-handed. The trick is not to ask too much from them at first. Then, once they've been collaborators for a while, they dare not disobey us lest we tell their comrades.

"Another good start is a sympathetic chat with a revolutionary whom we know is currently feeling aggrieved towards certain comrades. And then we give them a chance to get their own back. And how do we find revolutionaries who are feeling suitably aggrieved? We get existing secret collaborators to do things which will sow hurt or mistrust in the heart of a revolutionary whose assistance we particularly want. There's artistry to this, you know, Mr Holmes."

Colonel Volkhovsky paused, drew on the cigarette in his tortoiseshell holder and blew out a smoke ring. "Then, if they ever look like they'd like to actually lead revolutionary plots, these people get a sharp choice. Either they work with us and they'll be allowed enough successes to bring them fame, so they can attract revolutionaries to a gang under our surveillance. And we'll send their rivals to Siberia, or worse. Otherwise they go to Siberia themselves."

"Or worse," added Major Alexandrov, looking pleased with himself.

"Thank you, Major," said Volkhovsky. "To the many weaker souls among our collaborators," he continued, "the Okhrana can seem simply their source for money to fund a romantic nihilist layabout life, to be an exile in Paris, London or Zurich, or have their college fees paid, for we do a lot of that. They do not realise how much the little things we require in return are harming their revolutionary cause. They are pawns who do not see how their single square moves fit into the Okhrana's grand chess game.

"Then there are our bigger chess pieces, the secret collaborators who are active terrorists. They like to think that they are achieving more for their revolution, through us letting them continue as terrorists, than they are harming it through the help which we demand in return. We must help them believe they are cheating us successfully."

"There can be trouble if they ever discover how much harm their collaboration has done," said Major Alexandrov. "Their world falls apart. Sometimes they try to kill the Okhrana case officer who has been directing them. Sometimes they even kill themselves."

"Most of our secret collaborators like to believe they are still sincere revolutionaries," said Colonel Volkhovsky, "and the greater their apparent sincerity, the more that they are useful tools for us. And the most sincere and convincing agents of all are those who do not even realise they are being directed by the Okhrana. That is rather droll, don't you think, old chap?"

Volkhovsky suddenly sat up straighter in his chair, then continued: "That must be the end of this little peep show, Mr

Holmes, about the Okhrana's secrets. The curtain is now coming down and to delve any deeper, you must first sign up with us. And accompany Major Alexandrov along the winding corridors of our headquarters in St Petersburg."

"An experience you will never forget, Mr Holmes," said Major Alexandrov, grinning. "I think that, even for you, there will be at least one surprise. And, for light relief, our laboratories are right after your heart – invisible inks, deciphering codes, forensic chemistry and photography, and so much more."

"Have no worries about our *agent provocateur* methods, Mr Holmes," declared Volkhovsky brightly, "We stand for Empire, Property and Order every bit as much as this splendid Club here," He rubbed his hands and contemplated Holmes for a moment.

He leaned forward and smiled: "Rise above the common man's prejudice against the Okhrana, Mr Holmes. Our methods make the greatest chess game in the world and I sense that you in particular would find it stimulating to play. It is chess with a board of unbounded size and with humans as the pieces. And, as for the players," he now spoke very softly, "I can tell you it makes one feel like a god."

"I too feel that you belong with us, Mr Holmes, from everything I have read about you," said Major Alexandrov. "At last you would be among your true intellectual equals - with all the mental stimulation which that brings."

I could feel my blood boiling. At his last remark, Alexandrov had cast a quick disparaging glance towards me.

"Join us gods in the Okhrana and make common men your chess pieces," said Colonel Volkhovsky. "For, after this case, we may have some enthralling work for you in Britain. If Pryde-Anderson can persuade his colleagues, the Okhrana's methods may become By Appointment To Her Majesty Queen Victoria. In confidence, this is what we are advising him on.

"He is especially interested in how trade unions or parliamentary political parties can be secretly steered by secret police agents just like we steer underground revolutionary groups. In Russia our brilliant chief, Sergei Zubatov, has now shown how trade unions can be successfully set up and controlled entirely by the Okhrana, so genuine trade unions can't get a look in. In Russia, we are now scheming to create a parliament, just like your British one, but where all parties' leaders will be Okhrana secret collaborators. So government will look freer, but Okhrana power will be even greater.

"You, Mr Holmes, may possess that special combination of imagination and cunning which is needed to craft such schemes for Britain."

"Mr Holmes," interjected Major Alexandrov eagerly, "the secret political policeman is the man of the future. We are becoming the puppet-masters of governments. In joining us you would be embracing an idea whose time has truly come. It would be the most thrilling phase of your career."

"And to make a start," said Colonel Volkovsky, "you only need to reveal everything you know about the Liberty House case, then Major Alexandrov will arrange First Class travel to St Petersburg."

The grandfather clock struck the hour. For a moment, no-one spoke.

"Gentlemen, it is getting late," said Holmes, slowly rising to leave. "Indeed these are exciting prospects and you have given me rich food for thought. But I must now digest the latter and absolutely cannot decide here and now whether to join you. However, be assured that I am truly fascinated by everything you have told me. And I would truly love to visit the famous Okhrana laboratories. Within three days, I pledge, I will reply."

The three men smiled in turn at each other. I was not sure why, but never in my long partnership with Sherlock Holmes had I felt quite so alone.

*   *   *

As we stepped out of the Club and into the darkness of St James Square, Holmes said he wished to walk the whole way back. Walking would help him think through what to do next. At first we walked in silence through the November night mist.

The shock of the proposition from the Okhrana was foremost in my mind. Whatever Holmes decided, under no circumstances would I accept this imperious summons to St Petersburg. Then my sense of fear and foreboding revived. I worried about the need for urgent action before Pyotr Bogdanovich could launch any terrorist attacks. At least the Okhrana should be a powerful ally. We would not be on our own with this ghastly case.

As we turned off Piccadilly, I felt a sudden jolt of anxiety as three coaches full of policemen galloped past fast. Had the gang struck somewhere already? Should we not be heading straight to Scotland Yard ourselves?

In Savile Row, as we passed the darkened tailors' shops, Holmes at last spoke.

"What dreadful dilemmas, Watson. Protecting the public. Saving Angela Simmonds from the gallows and her sister from lifelong torment and infamy. Dealing with Pryde-Anderson's request. Warning Count Kropotsky. How can one combine these things? And whom can one trust and believe? How, indeed, have the Okhrana so rapidly found out that I am working on this case? And yet I simply must take some sort of action – and urgently."

After a few paces in silence Holmes halted beside a military tailor's dark shop window. In the dim gaslight from a street lamp, the face of a tailor's dummy in a naval officer's mess jacket looked strangely like Major Alexandrov.

"Watson, I hope you don't think I'm going to Russia. I was simply seeking to delay for some days the Okhrana's next move in this case, make them wait for my decision. Before they asked us to St Petersburg, everything they said was plausible. That we should combine forces on this case. That I have some inside knowledge about this gang – this afternoon we certainly got some. But how does the Okhrana want to use my help? To send us far away from London, the place where we could be most useful.

"In truth, the reason they have pulled strings with Pryde-Anderson to enlist me is to get me off this case. I sense one of their dark chess games in progress. I am a piece which has appeared inconveniently on their chess board. They want to know how I got there and what I have found out. But, after that, they want me off their chess board."

Holmes strode onwards once more.

As we crossed Oxford Street, I broke the silence.

"Holmes," I asked tentatively, "if The Organisation has infiltrated the Okhrana and uncovered its collaborators in London, how can we be sure that these two Okhrana officers are not in fact working for The Organisation? This strategy of the Okhrana, whereby the secret police themselves support terrorist gangs, could become frightfully dangerous, couldn't it, if genuine terrorists infiltrate the secret police? They could get a completely free hand for the most terrible plots – and government money to fund them and even the help of friendly governments like our own."

"Very true, Watson, and well-noticed. That is one of two dark and dreadful possibilities which we must now keep in mind at all times in this case."

So fraught was I now feeling, that I could not bear to ask Holmes what was the other possibility.

*   *   *

I spent a most restless night, sleeping fitfully. As I passed in and out of half-sleep, yet another fear was gradually crystallising in my mind, till I awoke sharply with my eyes open.

Surely the London Okhrana officer, who had sent the letter to Ivan Myshkin, might be one of the pair whom we had just met? If The Organisation's sources inside the Okhrana could learn of the briefcase, could they not likewise hear about our meeting? If The Organisation were planning attacks in London, would not a shrewd first move be to silence anyone on their trail? Lying awake in the early hours, it suddenly seemed blindingly obvious where might seem a logical first port of call for Bogdanovich's nihilist gang with their revolvers, axes, and bottles of home-made explosive.

It was 221B Baker Street.

Chapter 6: Day Of The White Mist

I never got a moment to share my fears with Holmes. When I saw the grim expression on his face next morning, I knew that something terrible had already happened. By the time I had risen for breakfast, Holmes was evidently already up and out. It was mid-morning when I heard his firm step on the stairs, returning. As he entered our sitting room, I could see from his face that something was wrong.

"Bogdanovich's terror attacks have started," he pronounced. He raised a copy of the morning paper. 'Russian philanthropist assassinated' was the headline.

"Early yesterday evening, Count Kropotsky was shot outside his home in Hampstead," Holmes announced. "The paper says that he had received an urgent warning of danger that very afternoon. He had packed to flee and was actually being helped by his secretary into his coach when four Russian exiles arrived and demanded a meeting about funding for a revolutionary group.

"The secretary refused and told the coachman to drive off. One attacker shattered the secretary's skull with a length of heavy chain and they then ran after the coach, firing with revolvers.

"A bullet penetrated the coach, hitting the Count who bled to death hours later. The gang ran off down Haverstock Hill, firing shots wildly at the windows of nearby houses."

Holmes looked at the newspaper. "It says he was 72 years old and," he read from the paper, " 'a leading liberal figure in the Russian exile community, known for organising funds to help Russian political exiles throughout Europe. He has been repeatedly accused by the Russian government of assisting violent revolutionary organisations through his various charities. His murder is expected to be presented by the Russian government as demonstrating the perils of befriending Russian exiles.' "

He passed the paper over to me.

"Who gave the Count the warning? Curious timing, don't you think, Watson? The warning was not sent till some five days after the story about him and the Okhrana surfaced at Liberty House. But just hours after that story reached our ears. First the Okhrana somehow hear about us, and now this warning. One is feeling rather spied on."

But Holmes seemed strangely composed as he said this.

Then he sighed deeply. "I've taken a desperate step this morning. It's the only move I can see which might break this case. I'm trying to get Pyotr Bogdanovich to come to," Holmes paused, his face clouded over, "a meeting."

I could not believe my ears. At that moment, Pyotr Bogdanovich sounded like the most dangerous person one could possibly encounter.

"It's a long-shot tactic to tempt him to show his face on his own," said Holmes. "At New Eden, Grigori told me how Nechaev fooled many revolutionaries through messages from fictitious revolutionary organisations on letterheads which he had created himself with a children's printing kit.

"So I got myself a John Bull Printing Outfit. And an hour ago I sent to Bogdanovich at Liberty House a written invitation from the 'World Revolutionary Command' to a meeting on a marked bench in the main avenue in Regents Park at two o'clock today.

"I told him that the Command might offer funding for a revolutionary so promising as himself. It's in English of course but Grigori said he understands English quite well.

"It's a desperate ploy. Bogdanovich may not even be at Liberty House, what with his activities last night. He may be suspicious. But he may be tempted by the money. After all, yesterday he tried to get money from Kropotsky and failed in a rather final way.

"Oh, and before I handed the letter to a cabbie to take round, I called on Victoria Simmonds to read it out to her so she's assured that I am taking energetic action."

"Good heavens, Holmes, you have been busy indeed," I replied.

"Will you come with me to this rendezvous in Regents Park, Watson? You're to observe from the undergrowth. You will need the nearest thing that you possess to gardening clothes, a notable gap in your wardrobe. And your revolver."

* * *

It was with a heavy sense of fate and duty that I accompanied Holmes. A white November mist was getting thicker as we strode out from Bakers Street towards Regents Park. He wanted to be in position a full hour before the meeting. By the time we reached the Park's central avenue the white mist was dense. We seemed completely alone there.

Holmes had everything planned. He had marked the bench for the meeting with a red ribbon and had stated this in the letter to Bogdanovich. It was three benches along from a path which intersected the central avenue. At the intersection was a bed of thick shrubs. Holmes led me through these shrubs. Crouched behind the shrubs, I had a good view of the meeting place and could watch the central avenue as far as the mist permitted. Then to my great surprise, Holmes climbed in beside me.

"But I thought you were meeting Bogdanovich on the bench?" I whispered.

"If my calculations are correct, that will prove unwise. We must be quiet now."

Only one walker passed through the white haze during our long, cold wait. At last two o'clock chimed in the distance. But the bench remained empty. How much longer did Holmes expect us to stay? And whatever for?

Five minutes later, down the avenue from the Zoological Gardens, a second walker came into view. My heart began to pound. It was a large, heavy set, bearded man with long black hair, wearing a long dark coat. And he was glancing at each bench. It was surely Pyotr Bogdanovich. Then he shambled towards the marked bench and sat down in the cold mist.

We crouched amid the shrubs. Bogdanovich sat on the bench, facing away from us. Nothing happened.

What were we waiting for? Whatever could happen? I looked quizzically at Holmes but he remained silent, finger on lips.

Still nothing happened.

Then after no more than ten minutes Pyotr Bogdanovich rose to leave. He began walking back along the avenue closer towards us.

At that moment, in the mist behind Bogdanovich, a strange, diffuse ball of cold-white light became visible down the path, like a will o'wisp. It rapidly grew larger and nearer to us. It grew and glowed like some spectral radiance.

Swiftly the entity emerged out of the mist. It was simply a bicyclist with a carbide and water lamp casting a cold bright glare from its tiny acetylene gas flame, diffused by the thick white mist.

The bicyclist slowed, overtook Bogdanovich, then stopped, dismounted and rested the bicycle against the bench nearest to us, then turned to face him. It was a youth, no it was a slim young woman. She began to speak to Bogdanovich and he replied.

Suddenly her right arm thrust out towards him. There was a bright flash and a loud pistol shot echoed out. Bogdanovich lurched back. She fired a second time, into his massive frame He then began to slowly totter forwards, advancing on her. She stepped back and fired a third shot directly into his chest. Slowly he dropped forward to his knees, coughing forth blood.

I reached for my revolver but Holmes held my arm down. "Wait!" he hissed.

The bicyclist was carefully scanning along the paths in all directions, her revolver levelled, looking for anyone coming through the mist.

As she looked away, Pyotr Bogdanovich somehow dragged himself upright. With his right hand he seemed to be trying to draw a pistol from his coat pocket. With a roar, coughing out blood, he lunged out and grabbed his assailant's left arm with his left hand. But she jerked her arm deftly and spun round balletically, causing him to hurtle head first on to the paving. His revolver skidded across the paving stones.

He slowly rose on to all fours and grasped towards his revolver on the ground. But his assailant had already taken aim. Her pistol flashed again and she shot him straight through the head. Bogdanovich collapsed face down, as if pole-axed, a dark red river of blood spreading out from his mouth.

I thought I could hear the sound of a police whistle in the distance. The young woman again scanned round, revolver levelled. Then she turned back and stepped across the prostrate Pyotr Bogdanovich.

She straightened her arm and aimed directly at the back of his head. Her revolver flashed and a fifth loud shot echoed out, point blank into the back of his head.

Swiftly she placed her revolver inside her coat, remounted her bicycle and pedalled on to the path besides which we were hiding. There now were definitely police whistles from the Zoological Gardens side of the Park. The Park Constables must have heard the shots.

"Quick," I whispered, "She'll have only one bullet left in her revolver. Shall we try to capture her?"

"Leave it," hissed Holmes.

Next she was bicycling rapidly down a path towards Chester Gate, really extremely fast. She was already once more just a glowing ball of diffuse white light in the mist, becoming smaller and smaller in the distance.

Holmes stood up: "Now you understand my reluctance to sit on that bench."

"But who was that? And how did she find him? And why?" I exclaimed.

"No time now. Let's get out of this park fast before anyone sees us," said Holmes, "lest questions get raised about our role in this. Thank goodness for this mist."

Chapter 7: 'Is That Enough Truth, Mr Holmes?'

We headed eastwards from Regents Park. Holmes hailed a hansom cab and directed it to Victoria Simmonds' address. Inside the cab we both relaxed. I felt overwhelming relief that the sinister driving force behind the Liberty House gang was now destroyed. A quiet sense of triumph emanated from Holmes.

"Now let us see if the other pieces to the puzzle fall into place," he said. "At last I am going to look behind that strangely placed Indian tapestry in Miss Simmonds' living room. For there is a moment of truth awaiting me concerning my understanding of this case.

"Do you remember how, when we first visited Victoria Simmonds at her home, she said she did not have at hand the note in Russian which Sophia had left with her for Anna Perovskaya? What struck me was that she then made no attempt to look for it even though we were actually in her apartment, where presumably the note must be. Unless, that is, she had already given it to someone else since her first contact with us.

"But to whom on earth might she have given such an important note? Surely only to the intended recipient herself.

"So had Anna Perovskaya unexpectedly arrived between our first two meetings, but sworn Victoria Simmonds to secrecy? After all, Sophia had appeared unexpectedly at Miss Simmonds' flat the day before our first meeting, so maybe Anna Perovskaya on the day after.

"So, if you remember, I then floated the idea of her impersonating Anna in a note to Angela Simmonds. That produced such a guarded response from her that I wondered if that oddly arranged Indian tapestry and dressing table were concealing the doorway to an adjoining room, where Anna Perovskaya might actually be listening to us. A door between two sets of bookshelves is quite common in such houses.

"So, if you remember, I next proposed the idea of me seeking out, there and then, a hidden listening place for myself in her apartment, if she were to invite her sister there. And that idea got a very frightened response from her indeed. Later, I observed her apartment from the street at night and saw signs that someone else might be present.

"So, ever since, I have been haunted by the notion that, whenever I am talking to Victoria Simmonds in that room, I may possibly also be talking to a leading Russian revolutionary listening behind that Indian tapestry. And that includes my earlier visit today to read out my note to Bogdanovich in front of Miss Simmonds. Some of my remarks, frankly, have been for the benefit of that imagined listener. So does she exist? Today, Watson, we will look behind that curtain."

We dismounted from the hansom cab in Bedford Square and soon Holmes was striking the knocker on Miss Simmonds front door. After some delay, it opened on a chain. When Victoria Simmonds saw that it was us, she opened wide. There was something obviously lighter, happier, brighter about her demeanour. We entered the hallway.

"Miss Simmonds," said Holmes at once quite loudly. "I need to negotiate with Anna Perovskaya immediately and everyone's problems can be solved. Can we meet in her listening place?"

The brightness was suddenly wiped off her face. "I don't know what you're talking about, Mr Holmes. I haven't seen her for months," she countered in alarm.

"I need to talk with Anna without that curtain between us and everyone's problems can be solved," declared Holmes loudly, then paused.

Suddenly a door opened in the rear end of the corridor and a young woman strode forward: "I will talk to Holmes," she said.

She was of strikingly beautiful looks - curly shoulder-length blonde hair, high Slavic cheek bones, and dazzling blue eyes. There was something masculine in her stance and in her clothes, a blue jacket and rough trousers and boots.

Then my heart pounded as I saw the fresh bloodstains on one boot and noticed how her right hand was thrust into the side pocket of her jacket. At last the penny dropped for me about how the assassin of Pyotr Bogdanovich had found him.

She walked close towards Holmes and looked at him very coolly. "How nice at last to see the face behind the voice," she declared boldly. "I have just been telling Victoria how you never turned up for the meeting with Pyotr Bogdanovich, which I overheard you planning. But that I met him instead and reached a deal whereby Angela will leave his revolutionary band and come with me to Zurich."

She was looking closely into his eyes.

"Yes," said Victoria, "it's simply wonderful. Anna's somehow persuaded Pyotr to tell Angela to go with her to Switzerland where she can start a new life."

"I would hazard that Anna used precisely five arguments, some for the heart and some for the head," said Holmes, glancing towards her.

Anna Perosvskaya's blue eyes flashed with alarm. She paused, silent. "Mr Holmes, we need to talk in private," she then declared. "Victoria, go to your bedroom please."

It was our client's home but there was no doubt who was in charge.

The Russian woman, Holmes and I entered the front room. Holmes strode over to the Indian tapestry and pulled it down. Behind it was indeed a doorway into a second room, the door slightly open.

"Forgive me," he said, "but by now I find that curtain rather distracting."

"I believe we can reach a deal," Holmes said to Anna Perovskaya. "We have a common interest in leaving the police out of this and in going our separate ways." She was looking at him warily. Her right hand was still deep inside the side pocket of her jacket.

"I will keep silent from everyone, Victoria included, about what we saw you do in Regents Park this afternoon," Holmes told her. "For two things in return. First that you take Angela Simmonds out of this country and help her build a life somewhere safe from justice, just like you have told Victoria."

A sudden look of great relief passed over the Russian woman's face. "That truly is what I am planning and what I now earnestly want. When you arrived, I was writing a note instructing Angela to meet me. She will heed me. In Zurich I have many helpers. I have already enquired about steamers to Boulogne."

"The other thing I want is truth," said Holmes. "There are puzzles still unsolved for me. Why did you kill Pyotr Bogdanovich? Why did you return to London in secret and hide here? Who warned Count Kropotsky? And why is it only now that you are telling Angela to come away with you?"

Anna Perovskaya was now looking at us with a puzzled expression. Perhaps she could not believe that escape was now so simple. I was relieved to see that both her hands were now resting in her lap. She was looking backwards and forwards between Holmes and myself.

Then slowly, solemnly she began to speak.

"I executed Pyotr because it was my duty as a revolutionary," she pronounced. "Let me explain. I was travelling to Tallinn within the Russian Empire – on some revolutionary business which does not concern you. But I was not alone. I had taken with me poor Sophia as my helper. We had sailed to Hamburg, then travelled overland to Lubeck where we were waiting to take a second steamer east along the Baltic to Tallinn. Sophia and I were visiting the cafés of old Lubeck, trying the famous Lubeck marzipan.

"Then Sophia started talking about how she longed now to travel everywhere with me as my assistant. But how there was something on her conscience which first she needed to confess to me. She told me that she had been working for the Okhrana.

"As a revolutionary, when I am told that directly, I have heavy responsibilities because it is often punishable by death. I interrogated Sophia and she told me how it had started.

"One day in St Petersburg, the Okhrana secretly arrested her in an alleyway on her way home from the university. They told her that her brother had just been captured with revolutionary pamphlets and would be tried and sent to a prison camp in Siberia. But the Okhrana could get charges dropped if she would give them just a little, unimportant help. Both of them could be released at once and no-one would ever know. When she hesitated, they said they would take her straight to her brother's cell and she could decide in front of him. At that, she gave in.

"For a year she was asked simply to send the Okhrana written reports on student meetings and was surprised to be paid quite well for this.

"Then the Okhrana suddenly offered to pay her university fees for a whole new course if she would spend just six months in London, all travel and living expenses paid. She was to report on Russian exiles' meetings to an Okhrana officer in London."

"Did you learn his name?" interrupted Holmes.

"It was Major Alexandrov," she replied. "He sent her to seek a bed at Liberty House and then met her weekly for reports on what went on there. So I questioned her on everything she had done for them.

"And then she told me something which chilled me. He had told her that another Okhrana collaborator had brought him a briefcase, containing secret documents, from its hiding place at Liberty House. He had now read these documents, so he said, and wanted her to return the briefcase to its hiding place, as if untouched. He gave her a locked leather briefcase and told her to hide it, yes, under the floorboards of the dressmaking room at Liberty House. An easy place to take up floorboards because it's so rarely used. He asked her to draw a plan of where she had put it so, he told her, he could check that it was the right place.

"Immediately I could see danger. I feared Alexandrov was planting evidence of crime to be discovered by the British police after a tip-off. Everything which Ivan and I had been planning at Liberty House might then be destroyed.

"I told Sophia my fears. And that we must return to London immediately so she could remove the briefcase and I would examine it. It was a most uncomfortable journey back together, I can tell you. When we got back, I stayed the night in a hotel. I told Sophia to go to Liberty House, then report back to me here, at Victoria's apartment, where I intended to arrive later. If Liberty House had already been raided by the police, I did not want to get arrested by policemen waiting for visitors – as happens in Russia.

"As we now know, we were too late. And it was not a police raid which the Okhrana had been engineering but false evidence that Ivan Myshkin and Count Kropotsky were working for them.

"And what absurd evidence! Both the Okhrana and Ivan were masters of codes and invisible inks. The Okhrana would never send a genuine letter like that and Ivan would never have so carelessly kept it. And I know for certain that the fabled Nechaev Organisation has never, ever existed and that any messages from it mean some trickery is going on.

"The Okhrana must have somehow sent a message about this briefcase to Pyotr Bogdanovich and were tricking him that this message was coming from The Organisation. This was their way to destroy both Ivan and Count Kropotsky here in Britain, without themselves breaking any British laws, by falsely making them out to be Okhrana collaborators.

"Imagine how Sophia would have felt when she found that she had brought about the murder of two people whom she had been living with. And I would now discover the terrible harm she had caused. And maybe the Okhrana might now use her deed to blackmail her to commit further hellish crimes. I think that she could not live with herself any longer."

"Yes," said Holmes slowly, "that at last makes sense of why Sophia threw herself under that train."

"Ivan was an important pillar of our armed struggle, an unrivalled planner," declared Anna Perovskaya, looking extremely grave. "Count Kropotsky was even more important. He got our cause a hearing in Britain and inspired the donations which make possible our resistance movement outside Russia.

And concerning Count Kropotsky, yes, it was me who warned him as soon as I heard about that false letter with which the Okhrana hoped to provoke attacks on him.

"The Okhrana have taken much trouble planning this," she continued. "With that letter of theirs, they even sacrificed one of their real spies in the group, poor wretched Boris, because they guessed he'd confess and thus make their plot look true.

"I do not know how they tricked Pyotr about the briefcase but he could be tricked quite easily, Mr Holmes. Look how he fell for your note to him today. He would believe anything which made him feel important."

She thought that Bogdanovich probably genuinely believed that he was being contacted by Nechaev's Organisation. She felt sure that the Okhrana had themselves arranged his famous escape from prison, hoping some day to make use of such a wild, destructive revolutionary. He had gone round telling people, she said, that his mysterious saviours had given him a code which The Organisation would subsequently use in messages to him. The Okhrana could easily have used this in a message to him about the briefcase, she said.

Anna Perovskaya was now animated and forceful and seemed suddenly keen to share her viewpoint with us. I could feel something of her fabled charm, I must confess.

She was talking more and more to me, her blue eyes flashing, for Holmes was now half turned away, chin in hand as if brooding on something. But what could be preying on his mind?

Anna Perovskaya said that her ears had pricked up when Victoria had mentioned Angela's remark about Pyotr's message from The Organisation to offer to work for the Okhrana. "That might neatly trick him into knowingly co-operating with the Okhrana in the future," she declared, "while still believing himself their fiercest opponent. Imagine what a whirlwind of horror Pyotr could have unleashed under Okhrana protection and direction! After whatever crimes in London, I feared the Okhrana would help him escape back to Russia, to launch mad acts of mass terror which would turn the public against us. And Pyotr would readily attack my own leaders too. He always wants to outdo other revolutionaries and wage war on them unless they totally worship him."

Holmes seemed more attentive now, his lips pursed as if poised to interrupt.

"Now this is a hard thing to share with you," she continued in full flow, "but Pyotr could have drawn quite a following. Like moths are drawn to a flame, there are all too many revolutionaries who will turn to a leader like him, whoever seems the fiercest, most ruthless. Imagine, someone as hate-filled and furious as Pyotr gaining a following because the

Okhrana plotted conflict between revolutionaries! So I had to put an end to him."

Holmes suddenly raised his hand, palm forward, at last cutting her short. He gazed straight ahead, then pronounced slowly:

"I do not doubt a word of all that. But answer me this. Surely the Okhrana needed to be certain that Sophia and, indeed, yourself would be far away from Liberty House when this briefcase was discovered. Sophia might easily have blurted something out if she had been present. As you've just said, you could have ridiculed the idea that this uncoded letter could be genuine.

"So what took you both so far from Liberty House at the crucial moment? What was this revolutionary mission in Tallinn and why on earth would you need to have Sophia with you? And why did you lie so low in London after you returned, when you have so much influence among revolutionaries?"

Anna Perovskaya's animation drained from her face, which then stilled completely, suddenly pale. Her right hand then slowly snaked back inside her jacket side pocket. She gazed blankly at Holmes for a moment. Then first came a quick look of hate, then across her beautiful face other emotions seemed to flit: bewilderment, fear, grief.

"I seek to understand the whole truth," said Holmes more gently. "And this is the last thing which I will ask from you. There is nothing you can do with that pistol which would not make it vastly harder to escape. And you recognise this, which is why you are talking to us at all. Whereas a few words revealing the whole truth, and that is the end of it. And I think you know what I am deducing."

She sat there frozen, silent.

Holmes continued, still soft and gentle. "Maybe you are aware that Dr Watson here writes up my cases for eventual publication. If you share the whole truth, I give my word of honour that Dr Watson's record will not be published for 100 years. Whereas if you stay silent, it will be published no later than other cases and it will make public my suspicions."

She was still silent, looking from one of us to the other. She seemed as if in pain. She seemed now so different from the confident young woman who had greeted us in the corridor, let alone the ruthless, straight-shooting assassin who had killed Pyotr Bogdanovich.

"Please," said Holmes, "I simply need to understand for my own sake, not to judge. "

She stared ahead for a moment. Then her right hand fell back to her side.

"You may find this hard to understand," she began. "But a price for being a leader in our revolutionary struggle is that you must do some work for the Okhrana or they will not let you be. It is like a tax. Then you can get on with your real work.

It was something which I found I had to do if I was to achieve anything at all. If you do not pretend to help them, they can so easily get you sent to Siberia. Whereas for a little token help to the Okhrana, you can organise fairly openly and do them far more harm than they ever suspect. I can travel in and out of Russia for instance and I use that to great effect. Whereas, if I had been jailed in Siberia, my talents, my talents...", her voice sounded suddenly tremulous and faltering, "all my talents for the revolution would have gone to waste. Mr Holmes, you have no idea how many people I have awakened to join our revolutionary cause. But I can only use these talents if I stay free."

She paused, regaining her composure, then declared: "It was my revolutionary duty to seize the opportunities which work for the Okhrana can bring, however unpalatable from a self-centred bourgeois viewpoint.

"Our journey to Tallinn was on instructions from the Okhrana. My case officer – he's the head Okhrana man in London – told me to instruct Sophia to come with me to Tallinn. He told me he wanted me to introduce her to a revolutionary group there.

"Now that seemed well within the price which I pay the Okhrana for working unhindered. After all, I would do other things for our cause on this journey. And, most certainly, I would secretly tell the leader of the Tallinn group that I had suspicions that Sophia was an Okhrana collaborator. And that could make her a sort of asset for them because she could be carefully fed false information. And the Okhrana may stop trying to place other spies in the group, once they think they have infiltrated it. You have to understand how all this works, Mr Holmes.

"It's strange, I know. We take three steps forward, working for the revolution. Then two steps back, working for the secret police. But that leaves us one more step ahead each time. And eventually we make progress with a plot which they have not infiltrated. And we have killed one Czar already and surely will kill another.

"Take our plot for Angela to become a tutor in a Grand Duke's household in St Petersburg – I do not think the Okhrana ever discovered this, despite having spies actually living at Liberty House. It was known only to Ivan and Angela - and myself, since I found Angela for Ivan, who had asked me to find a British teacher for this purpose. And who knows where we might have got with this plot? Angela might have ended up tutoring within the Winter Palace itself. And she might have done more there, who knows, than simply spy."

She paused and looked hard at Holmes, her face very solemn. Then she continued.

"So, anyway, I was taking Sophia to Tallinn on Okhrana instructions, thinking that she must either already be an Okhrana collaborator or was due to be turned into one soon. And then she confessed to me. But, when she told me about the briefcase, that changed everything. I worried that Okhrana's real purpose for our journey was to get us both away from London, so something truly terrible could happen at Liberty House. So I rushed back."

She looked straight ahead and spoke sadly: "When I discovered what the Okhrana had engineered at Liberty House, I felt my case officer, Colonel Volkhovsky, had completely betrayed the understanding which I thought we had together. I determined that I would smash their plot.

"But I worried that the Okhrana might expose and destroy me next. That's why I did not want anyone to know I was back in London. Once one Okhrana collaborator is exposed, all the others worry that it could happen to them too. I think that's why Katya ran off from Liberty House - I've long suspected that she was the Okhrana's main spy there. Indeed the Okhrana would not have sacrificed Boris Burtliev unless they still had another spy there.

"When I heard from Victoria that she had already engaged you, I was furious. I considered ordering her to dismiss you. But I feared that you might contact Scotland Yard, if suddenly dismissed. So I wondered if, instead, I could make use of the great Sherlock Holmes. I needed to find out what had happened at Liberty House, because Sophia's note to me only repented for what she had done. I forced Victoria, I'm afraid, only to see you right here where I could listen to everything which you were discovering.

"Then I thought of another way to make use of you. I sent a well-disguised anonymous note to Colonel Volkhovsky simply telling him that you were on the case. I wanted to worry the Okhrana that Sherlock Holmes was on their trail, make them feel watched, make them hesitate and fear to go further with their plot. I hoped you could be a card in my hand.

"When you came this morning and read aloud your letter to Pyotr, I had already been considering that same old ploy of a letter from a fictitious organisation to get him somewhere on his own. But that trick could only be played on him once, so it was now or never.

"And then you read to Victoria from the newspaper about the murder of poor Count Kropotsky, who has done so much for our cause. I decided I must kill Pyotr on his way back from meeting you and save our people from further harm.

"When it seemed that you were not coming and Pyotr was leaving the bench, I took my chance. As for Colonel Volkhovsky, revolutionary justice will certainly come." She struck her bulky right-hand pocket with her hand.

Her tough, confident persona seemed back, as she made her threat against Colonel Volkhovsky. "Is that enough truth, Mr Holmes?" she asked. "I need to act fast to get Angela away from Liberty House before any police call there. That loud, wild Bogdanovich will have attracted enough attention for police descriptions of his corpse to obtain information about where he was living."

"It's enough truth," said Holmes softly, "It's enough."

Chapter 8: Aftermath

It was New Year's Eve, several weeks later, and Holmes and I were having afternoon tea at Baker Street. Outside, a snow-laden sky, heavy grey with almost a dull yellow tinge, was releasing first flurries of snowflakes over the red brick chimneystacks. In our snug sitting room, we were enjoying a pot of fine Darjeeling tea and warm buttered crumpets, toasted with forks on the fire.

Holmes was reflecting on the year which was now ending.

"Now that case of the Camden Town anarchist gang and the Russian secret police plot," he declared. "That is an experience which I would not wish repeated. The costs of any misjudgement were so particularly terrible. One felt so alone. I could not trust even my client, since early on I realised that she might be under someone else's control. I had so little to work with. Only the suspicion that there was someone secretly listening to our conversations and my plan to manipulate that person through what I said.

"Then, once I saw that those Okhrana officers actually sought to divert my investigation, I began pondering whatever they could be seeking to hide. And during their efforts to impress me with their cleverness and tempt me to join them, they unwittingly prompted me about things to look out for in this particular case.

"You know, the little boast about engineering escapes from prison in Russia. The crack about revolutionaries who are being steered by the Okhrana without realising it, and various other little asides. And they even had to crow about their codes and invisible inks, so signally unused in that damning letter.

"So thank you, gentlemen of the Okhrana, for demonstrating not only your intelligence but its limits."

Holmes paused and sipped from his delicate Chinese teacup and gazed towards the falling snow.

"How strange to think that we went through that ordeal so recently," he pronounced, "yet all has passed away quietly."

Victoria Simmonds had received a letter from her sister. Angela had successfully fled to Switzerland with Anna Perovskaya. They were living amidst the large Russian student community in Zurich.

In her apologetic letter thanking Holmes, Victoria Simmonds had mentioned that she had turned her back on foreign politics altogether. Instead, she was putting her energies into some sort of medical education work with impoverished young women in London's East End. Now, what with being a doctor and knowing the Simmonds sisters' attitudes, I had a presentiment about where this sort of thing might be heading.

The police had successfully connected Bogdanovich to Liberty House, which they had found deserted by its occupants. No arrests had been made nor had body parts been discovered there or on the Heath or in the Canal. And of course there was no police search for the latter, since the two murders at Liberty House were as yet unknown.

But Holmes thought it likely that tales of the murders would some day reach the police, since so many Liberty House residents had witnessed them. The latter were people likely to attract police investigation in any country, he said. Sooner or later, Holmes believed, one of them would disclose the story, in an attempt to obtain police leniency over something else.

Thus he believed that some day a British warrant would be issued for the arrest of Angela Simmonds for the murder of Ivan Myshkin. So he doubted that she could ever safely return to British domains.

"It was a frighteningly close thing but we achieved our goals," said Holmes. "We prevented ghastly terrorist outrages. And we saved our client's sister from the terrible consequences of her entry into this world of the damnable and the damned."
He stared out towards the snowflakes falling in the darkening sky. He seemed in a maudlin mood.

"From the most terrible of those consequences, I should rather say. For we did not enable two murderesses to flee to a cheery life of hero-worship among Russian students in Zurich.

Looking into a crystal ball, I would see only pain and trouble for both Angela Simmonds and Anna Perovskaya.

"Tell me, Watson, which would be the greater pain? For Angela Simmonds to believe that all along she had been deceived by Ivan Myshkin, after she had pledged her life to his cause? Or to discover instead that she misjudged him and herself destroyed the plans which they had shared? And how hellish might her relationship with Anna become if ever she suspects her heroine's secret link to the Okhrana!

"But must not Anna tell Angela that The Organisation's reappearance is a deception? So can she really avoid explaining that she killed Bogdanovich and why? But then might not Angela ask the same question as myself about why Anna took Sophia abroad just before the Okhrana sprang its trap?

"And other people will definitely come, asking that question. For Anna must report Ivan's murder to the Russian Socialist Revolutionary Fighting Force, who will investigate his disappearance anyway. They have their own investigations unit in Paris, Grigori has told me, for uncovering the Okhrana's secret collaborators. And sooner or later they will seek out both Anna and Angela, to check what really happened in this case."

Holmes gazed into the snowstorm. The rooftops on the other side of Baker Street were now covered in soft white snow. He continued: "Truth will most likely out eventually – and Anna Perovskaya probably recognises this and will take action in advance. Grigori told me about a revolutionary in a similar predicament who killed his own Okhrana case officer to make his final stand for the revolution. Then fled forever to the American West for a pioneer farmer's life in a sod cabin on the prairie.

"Anna Perovskaya might as well do likewise because I can see no better future for her now. This much admired Red Queen will have been driven off the Okhrana's chessboard for good."

Holmes shook his head. He could see no future for Angela either among Europe's community of wandering exiled revolutionaries. As tales spread, anyone linked to the dark events around Liberty House would become tainted with suspicion. He had now risen and begun to pace on the Persian carpet.

"What a ghastly world these revolutionaries inhabit," he mused aloud, "where the secret police proffer this Devil's Pact for collaborators. You are offered a charmed life - full of fervour, fame and thrills of revolutionary plotting but safe from the gallows or the living death of a Siberian prison camp.

"But in return you never know which of your comrades your deeds are sending to those very fates. Nor which of your grand plots are already known to the Okhrana and succeed only because they suit the Okhrana's purposes. Never do you know which of your comrades or, indeed, your leaders are also working for the Okhrana. And you never know when the Okhrana may break the bargain and effect your destruction.

"Oh, it is easy to see why Grigori is now making sandals and growing tomatoes at New Eden. For even sincere revolutionaries, like Grigori, can be caught in this dreadful Okhrana chess game. If your leader or your leader's leader is a pawn of the Okhrana, then you are a pawn too."

Holmes turned to me suddenly: " 'The Case of the Russian Chess Board'. That's what you should call this case, Watson, when you write it up, then seal the file for a century, as I promised Anna Perovskaya. An invisible chess board, but no less real."

I was tiring of Holmes' gloomy reverie and sought to change the subject. Had he heard more, I inquired, about Malcolm Pryde-Anderson's scheme to promote Okhrana methods in Britain, the scheme where Colonel Volkhovsky had tried to tempt Holmes with hints of a prestigious role.

"I asked about that at lunch with Mycroft just before Christmas," he replied. "He told me that Pryde-Anderson has sharply fallen from grace. It seems that he has absolutely no idea how to persuade the much older generals and admirals on his Working Party. He is much too full of himself and they deride him as a young whippersnapper.

"And they wish to keep at arms length his Russian advisers, whose true motives for sharing their secrets they deeply suspect.

"So the Working Party is ending inconclusively and Pryde-Anderson is to be transferred to review food costs in prisons instead."

Holmes sighed deeply, then continued.

"But Mycroft thinks that certain Working Party members are privately fascinated by what Pryde-Anderson has gleaned from the Russians and that, after a discreet interlude, they will advance them as if their own home-grown ideas.

"He says it's not so much the covert running of revolutionary groups which interests them, because Scotland Yard's new Special Branch already does this, it seems. It's the new Okhrana schemes for secretly steering political parties and trade unions.

"It seems that Pryde-Anderson revealed information from Volkhovsky about how the Paris Okhrana have been gaining influence in the French parliament. Initially they just wanted to manipulate the French to deport particular Russian exiles. But now they've found they can also steer French foreign policy towards Russia. It seems that secret police and ambitious members of parliament go together like horse and carriage."

"Pray explain," I asked.

"Volkhovsky told Pryde-Anderson that the Paris Okhrana were astounded at how French politicians would stop at nothing to line their own pockets or to stab a rival in the back. This makes them perfect as willing secret collaborators, as open to hire as a hansom cab.

"That's why the Okhrana are changing their tune on a parliament for Russia, like Volkhovsky told us. Because they now see they could do such easy business with the many greedy, corrupt people among those who'd seek to get elected."

"Did Mycroft grasp how all this works in Paris?" I inquired.

"The Okhrana gradually clear a path upwards for their favoured politicians by ruining their rivals, just like Volkhovsky told us concerning revolutionaries. In Paris the Okhrana use French private detectives, my very own opposite numbers," Holmes grimaced, "to uncover or fabricate scandals concerning their protégés' superiors or rivals. They then get these scandals publicised by favoured French journalists, whom they reward with bribes and exclusive stories.

"And these secret policemen can then call in favours from successful protégés in order to promote other ambitious politicians in their stable. And favoured deputies fast become junior ministers, then senior ministers. And the higher you get your man promoted, there are ever more strings he can pull for you. And he knows that he must keep doing you those favours, lest you ever do to him what you did to his rivals.

"And so he argues for the treaties you want and even lets you in on military secrets.

"Mycroft says some Working Party members are cock-a-hoop about all this. They are dreaming about how intelligence officers at British Embassies could obtain such influence in foreign countries, steer new alliances and generally pull strings.

"And they'd most certainly like the same within our own parliament, so they could steer any government and ruin any government which defied them. Not least, Mycroft says, they'd like to infiltrate this Keir Hardie chap's new Independent Labour Party, lest it ever become a force.

"And in their Clubs, he says, they are joking about how senior secret policemen could themselves 'retire' to become MPs," Holmes continued, "and draw on their organisation's power to advance their political careers. And Mycroft thinks the talk has lasted too long for it to end as jest. He hazards that some military intelligence operations with such proclivities may fairly soon appear."

"Do you think, Holmes," I asked, "that Mycroft might put in a quiet word somewhere about your special talents, if ever this does get started? As those Okhrana men told you, what a climax to your career to assist a secret, patriotic project of this importance!"

Holmes turned slowly towards me, a baleful expression in his eyes.

"Everything which I observed during that case makes me detest such a thought," he replied with a fervour which is rare in him. He clasped his hands tightly and continued:

"This secret policeman's dream of playing puppet-master over governments will foster such arrogant use of secret power just for its own sake. Remember how those conceited Okhrana men boasted to us about the thrill of playing god!

"I fear that these British would-be puppet-masters would turn out much the same. They will always say they know best for Britain and justify whatever tyranny, terror or torture makes them feel powerful. 'Think of Britain' said Pryde-Anderson when he bade me help the Okhrana, which would have let their foul plot flower. Thank goodness, for Britain's sake, that I followed my own judgement instead."

Holmes paused, looking out over the falling snow. He continued, but in a softer tone.

"And yet those Okhrana men were not wholly wrong when they said that I am of their kind. Playing their devious chess games would have a deep and dark appeal to my type of mind. For I am the lean and hungry type who must hunt and scheme and thrive on battle of wits. Thank Providence that I can satisfy these tiger instincts of mine by fighting such criminal schemes, not plotting them myself."

The End

Other MX Sherlock Holmes Titles

Short Fiction Collections

The Lost Stories of Sherlock Holmes

Outstanding Mysteries of Sherlock Holmes

Novels

Shadowfall

Barefoot on Baker Street

Rendezvous at The Populaire (vs The Phantom)

I Will Find The Answer (vs Dr. Jekyll)

A Case of Witchcraft

The Sign of Fear, A Study In Crimson (the adventures of the female Sherlock Holmes)

Sherlock Holmes and The Affair In Transylvania

Modern Fiction

No Police Like Holmes

Murder in the Library

The Case of the Grave Accusation

www.mxpublishing.com

Other MX Sherlock Holmes Titles (continued..)

Historical / Non Fiction

Close To Holmes

Eliminate the Impossible

The Norwood Author [winner 2011 Howlett Literary Award]

A Chronology of Sir Arthur Conan Doyle

Sherlock Holmes, Conan Doyle and Devon

Biographies

Watson's Afghan Adventure

In Search of Dr Watson

Bertram Fletcher Robinson

Special Collections

Baker Street Beat

and many more.........

www.mxpublishing.com

THE
OUTSTANDING
MYSTERIES
OF
SHERLOCK HOLMES

WRITTEN & ILLUSTRATED BY
GERARD KELLY

www.ingramcontent.com/pod-product-compliance
Lightning Source LLC
Chambersburg PA
CBHW071329130626
46556CB00004B/1813